DADDY CRUSH

A. ANDERS

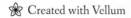 Created with Vellum

To the Diva Squad. Miss you.

CONTENTS

1

JUST ONE KISS

JERUSHA

I'm about to have my first kiss and I feel absolutely nothing. No excitement, no flutters, not even a glimmer of curiosity.

It's me. I'm sure of it, after more than a dozen dates. My fault, my problem. *Me.*

I twist out of my date's clammy hold and step away, putting my back to my front door. "Um, Jed, I think maybe—"

There's no time to avoid his swoop. My mouth's still open when we collide in a messy mix of teeth (mine) and tongue (his). I don't even think before shoving him off.

"*Yuck!*" I swipe a sleeve over the mess he's made of my face.

"You didn't like that?"

"I don't think I'm ready for—"

"What? Come on. Just a kiss."

"Seriously, I'm not—"

"Hey. I walked you home. At least invite me in." He pauses for a second before going on. "Come on, babe. Let me in. We'll see where this—"

"She said no." The low, rough voice comes out of nowhere

and I can tell it frightens my date. Relief floods me to the tips of my extremities.

"Excuse me?" Jed turns to peer into the dark.

Quick, decisive footsteps scuff down a set of wooden stairs, over a few feet of sidewalk, then up onto my porch. It's Karl, my neighbor. Like every other time I've seen him, something flops around in my belly, heavy and hot. So maybe it's not all me. Maybe I've been dating the wrong guys.

Maybe I should date Karl.

"Take off." Karl's tone leaves no room for argument.

"What?"

"She doesn't want to invite you in. She doesn't want you to touch her. Get out of here."

My date's chest puffs out before he fully takes my neighbor in. I can tell the second he realizes just how outclassed he is because he deflates, like a balloon. "Whatever, man."

I know it's not right, but something dark inside me wishes he wouldn't back down. I picture Karl's thick, ink-darkened hands grabbing Jed's lapels, imagine the way his back muscles would ripple if he threw him out into the street.

Here I go again, thinking ridiculous Karl thoughts at the worst possible moment. It happens every time he shows up. My insides get tense and achy and I want things I'd never thought to wish for. Right now, I'm out of breath, sick to my stomach, and so hot I want to shed my coat.

"Later, babe." Jed's clearly not looking for a fight. And that's fine. It's good. A fight would be an awful end to the evening. He flicks me a look, lifting his chin in a way that is supposed to be macho, but looks childish.

"Well, no," I reply. "Not later. I don't think..."

He's already gone, crunching down the leaf-strewn street toward the university.

"It's an expression," Karl tells me with a smirk. A second later, his lips tighten into a frown and one dark eyebrow lifts.

"Unless you want to see him again? You want me to call him back? Did I butt in when I shouldn't have?"

I shake my head, remembering the feel of Jed's slobber on my face and the fear that he wouldn't back down. I should go inside and wash him off, but I can't go anywhere while Karl's standing here. "Definitely not. Thank you, Karl."

"Another bad one, huh?"

"Wasn't great." My breath puffs out between us. It's cold, I notice, though I'm clammy-hot from my proximity to this man.

"You let this one walk you home?"

"I thought..." What did I think, exactly? That it wasn't too bad? That he wasn't a total jerk? I can't tell Karl what's running through my head because even I, in all my innocence, know that this line of thinking is pathetic: *He didn't gross me out, so I let him walk me home.* "I don't know. I was hopeful, I guess."

"Prick doesn't know how to kiss a woman goodnight." Karl shifts like he's about to leave and I can't let that happen. Everything I've been looking for in a man is right here. He's twice my age, fine, but that shouldn't matter. He's single—I think—and the way he makes me feel is like nothing I've experienced.

"Night, Jerusha." He turns to go, whistling low for Squid, who slides silently from the shadows of my porch. I've never seen a dog quite so quiet as this one. So stealthy, I hadn't seen him arrive.

"Wait."

Karl stops and looks at me, far enough out of my porch light's glow that his eyes are two dark holes in his wide, slavic face. There's the beginning of a beard on his chin and I tighten my hands into fists to keep myself from touching him there.

"You, um... You do this with all the neighbors?"

"This?" He glances out at the dimly-lit street with its trees and wonky sidewalks and the long line of row houses.

"Late-night front porch interventions."

He exhales. "You're the only one, Jerusha."

My "Oh," is more breath that voice.

Balanced on the edge of the top porch step, Karl stands like he's aching to leave, fingers agitated, body vibrating with pent up energy. What would it be like to see him let it all out, instead of holding it in? Colossal, I imagine. Explosive.

"How *should* he have done it?" I address his antsy silhouette, courageous now that his face is entirely in shadow.

He goes very still, head tilted at a curious angle. "Done it?"

"Kissed me good night."

"Not like that."

"But how?" Even in the dark, I can't keep my eyes from Karl's lips.

A car approaches, its lights skimming his back before it slows for the stop sign. It's like that outside presence pushes a button, releases him from his frozen position. He shifts down to the first step, putting a few more inches between us. "You, uh..." I can hear him swallow, the sound loud in the night. Everything's strangely still, reminding me of a film set. My porch right on the sidewalk, but so enclosed we might as well be inside. "Not something I can explain, you know? There's just a right and a wrong way and that was definitely the wro—"

"Show me." The words come bursting out, though I guess the idea's been there for a while. Maybe since the first time I saw Karl.

"Come again?"

"Show me how you kiss a woman goodnight."

He shakes his head in this quick little rhythm that I can't read in the dark. Is he as frantic as I am? Did my request turn his insides to jelly and make him want to turn around and hide? Suddenly, I hate the shadows. I need light to know just how badly I've messed things up with my nearest neighbor—the man whose house is literally stuck to mine, whose porch is so close I could climb over the railing and be there.

"Oh, gosh. I'm so sorry, Karl. You're just... I'm just..." I'm hot, face on fire, tears closer to the surface than I'd realized—not in my throat, but right there, burning my sinuses. "I'm a fool." An absolute fool, to think that the broody, kind, inked-up giant next door would want to show me *anything*. "I'll just go inside now and we can pr—"

He mutters something I don't understand and in two strides, he's here, above me, around me, his body so much bigger this close. He doesn't touch me, though. He must not want me to. I don't move an inch when his head lowers beside mine, putting his mouth to my ear.

"You've..." He clears his throat, though it clearly didn't work given how rough he sounds when he goes on. "Never been kissed?"

"No," I whisper, keeping every muscle stock still. "Except for tonight, with—"

"Doesn't count." His words are warm on the side of my face. *He's* radiating heat, this close. I want to touch him, to see if he's as hot as I am, if his skin burns the way mine does.

"Oh."

"Put your hands on me."

After a second's hesitation, I lift them like a zombie and stall out, hanging in midair. "Where?"

"Where would you like?"

My eyes go to town, flicking all over him. Endless possibilities assail me in a rush—rough face, hard chest, bulky shoulders. Is that short hair as spiky and stiff as it looks or would it give beneath my fingers? My attention lands on his hands. I think about those a lot—and not just in bed when I fantasize them onto my skin, but in class, while working, walking, on the bus. Pretty much all the time.

"Would you... Can I hold your hand?"

The pained noise that rattles deep in his chest tells me that I've gone too far.

"I'm sorry, I shouldn't..." I force a laugh that hurts coming out. "I'll, um. I should let you go home. Okay, Karl. Good night!"

Karl

"Jerusha."

She stops trying to get her key in the lock, but doesn't otherwise move.

"You okay?"

Quick nod. I don't believe it for a second. Her shoulders are so high and tight she looks ready to fly off.

"Give me your hand."

After a few excruciating seconds, she turns, head down. I'm waiting for her, palms up. She glances at me, all big, blue eyes and freckles and that soft, soft mouth, and something pings inside my chest, hard.

Slowly, she puts her hands on mine, light as, I don't know, butterflies landing on flowers or something. They're weightless, but warm. And just this barely there contact feels good. It's all I can do not to squeeze her, wrap her up, protect her from the shitty world.

I wait, breath held.

There's hardly any pressure; just that heat, until she lightly drags her palms back, putting our fingertips together, finally leaving our middle fingers to latch like hooks. It's the weirdest, softest, sweetest thing I've experienced in ages and it's twisted something in my chest.

I flick a glance up to her face to find it hidden behind a puff of messy brown hair. But I need to see her—confirmation that what I'm doing is okay. Because, hell, she's got to be a virgin—that's what the never been kissed thing means. I'm at least a decade older than her. Probably two. She's little and soft. I might break her.

"Tilt your head back," I whisper, instead of letting her go like I should. "Let me look at your face."

Her mouth's glistening, bottom lip indented for a second as though she's been biting it and I have to shove back a wave of ridiculous jealousy that I'm not the one doing the biting.

Nobody's getting bitten tonight. That's not what this is about. It's not about me being a horny bastard whose been hungering for my twenty-something virgin neighbor since she moved in six months ago. And she is cute, man. But no. This is about making sure her first kiss isn't some shitty mauling on her front porch.

One of her hooked fingers tugs at mine. I let her drag me closer, flashing back to the first time I saw her, cleaning this porch, with her long hair and long skirts and long pauses before talking, like she's thinking things through before letting them out. She smiled that day and I couldn't breathe for a few seconds. I headed off to work, wondering if there was a husband or boyfriend inside.

There's no reason that exchange should come back—or my response to her. Nothing happened that day beyond a *Nice to meet you, neighbor*. Well, and that stupid stab of curiosity. Fuck it —*envy*.

The fact is, there's something almost magic in the way I respond to her after so many years of feeling nothing.

"Will you do it?"

I blink back down at her face.

"Will you kiss me? Will you show me how it's done?"

My inner cynic's laughing his ass off. Where do I get off thinking I know a goddamn thing about women? With a track record like mine, this is the last thing I should be doing. And, yet...

Of all the pricks she's brought back after what seems like an endless string of dates, not one recognized how precious she is. Not one.

I do. I saw it that first goddamn day.

Guess that's enough for my conscience to give me the green light.

"Come here." I lean down, taking care not to touch her any more than I already am. I'm a bruiser. Doesn't mean I have to break what I touch. I get another flare of guilt at the reality—that I hurt a lot of people in my past life.

Not anymore. Not her.

Her breath's warm and smells like spices. Her exhales are kind of stuttery and, though it's ridiculous, especially considering the differences in our ages and sizes and histories, I like that I've managed to do that to her. She didn't seem jittery with that other guy. Just annoyed.

My hands itch to slide into that mass of hair and hold her still, but that's the last thing this woman needs. I rein that in and brush my nose against hers. Just a touch, but even that changes her breathing and, hell, my own.

I sense her mouth before I touch it—a sweet warmth that I'd dive into if I didn't have such a tight leash on myself.

And then it's too much, the denial, the way her breathing's picked up, the sway of her body toward mine. I let my lips land on hers. The contact practically sizzles.

My cock's heavy and warm and I haven't even tasted her yet. But I want to, dammit. I'd gladly trade a week's worth of food for a chance to get to know every inch of her skin.

Her head tilts, her plush mouth opens, her little tongue touches my lip and I'm gone.

Fuck me, I'm lost.

Jerusha

This is nothing like that other kiss—which wasn't a kiss. Not even in the same realm.

Funny how I know that now, after less than a second with Karl.

And it's not just what he's doing that's different, it's him. How he tastes, his smell up close, this presence all around me—overwhelming but not pushy. He's so tender, so careful, and yet I feel him everywhere—from the frantic flutter in my chest, down through my belly, to where I'm pulsing between my legs.

I open myself further, the way they do in the movies, and lean forward, barely aware that I'm on my tiptoes, giving him more, letting him in.

It takes a second to realize that his tongue isn't delving inside the way I've seen people do. His hands are nowhere on my body.

I force myself away, winding up with my back to my front door. My hands are tingling so hard, they're almost numb and I'm breathing fast like I've just run.

So is he, which is a relief, though nothing in his expression tells me if he liked this or if it was a duty he felt obligated to carry out. At least the breathing hard tells me he's affected.

I think.

I'm too worked up to be embarrassed, but I feel it there, trying to wind its way inside. "I'm sorry," I whisper, putting my fingers to my mouth as if to wipe him away, although that's the last thing I'll do. Instead, I press the pads to quiet the buzzing his touch left behind.

"Why?"

"For making you..." I swallow, recognizing how callow I've been to pressure him into doing this.

His laugh stops me short. "Making me?" He shakes his head and sucks in a long breath, looking off to the side, as if there's anything to see there but his dark front porch. "I'm twice your size. You couldn't make me do anything I didn't want to do."

The excitement starts right back up again. "You wanted to do that?"

His attention's back on me and it's heavy, intimidating. What would all that physical power feel like if he let himself go, instead of holding back?

"Wanted to do that since the first time I saw you."

"Why didn't you?"

He huffs out a laugh. "What? Grab you in the alley out back, shove you against the wall between the trash cans and…"

Please finish that sentence. Please tell me how hard you'd hold me. Tell me how you'd make me feel, how deep you'd kiss, how long you'd make me take it. Tell me what I taste like, because your taste is indescribable and I want more. "And what?" I'm breathless. Hoarse.

"Nothing." He shoves away from my door, backs up a step, another, and turns to leave. I want to stop him so badly it hurts. "Night, Jerusha."

That's it? He rips me right open, leaving nothing but an oozing puddle of want, and he's just going to take off, like none of this happened?

I open my mouth, wishing I had the gumption to demand he finish what he started. At the very least, I could ask why he's leaving. I've grown a backbone—or discovered it—these past few months, so I straighten up and let him go, but it's hard.

I manage a solid "Good night" and watch him lope off into the dark night, his dog at his side. Within a couple seconds, he's just another shadow.

2

TEMPTATION

JERUSHA

The next week's a mess of classes and late nights getting ready for my big art show. The piece I'm working on is calling me back to the studio, but my back hurts and my eyes are fuzzy and Karl doesn't work on Thursday nights.

I've got an excuse to go see him burning a hole in my pocket— a post card invitation to my first solo show. It's in the best gallery in town. I'm so excited I could burst.

I stop off for a pizza and make it a large, telling myself it's because I love leftovers, but the lie is thin. Especially when I add a six-pack of Modelo at the last minute. No denying what I'm doing. It's Karl's brand.

The invite, the pizza, his favorite beer. I remember that detail from the night we sat on his back stoop last summer and drank beer. He took me to Home Depot in his truck, where I bought lighting fixtures for my house. When we got back, I realized I didn't have a ladder tall enough to install the lights on the high first-floor ceilings, so he brought his and then stuck around to give me a hand.

The best thing that day, aside from sharing that beer, side by side, was the way he helped me, so different from anything I'd experienced back home. He didn't take over the project like my father or brothers would. He waited for me to lead, offering a hand, as needed. That level of deference, from such a big, stern-looking man had taken the threads of attraction I already felt and twisted them up into something stronger.

I think of him every time I look at my ceiling fans.

I practically skip the last couple blocks home now, excited at the prospect that I might see him and tell him my good news. Will he come to the opening? Maybe as my date?

I don't know. I've caught him watching me with a weird smile before...like he doesn't quite get me. Like maybe I'm a weird little person he can't wrap his mind around.

I force myself to slow at the last minute. Right. Gallivanting like a four-year-old probably isn't the best way to approach him. I can't quite manage a sedate walk, but I can go slow. Ish.

The streets are a restless jumble of whirling wind and fallen leaves. People give me more of the looks I've gotten used to since moving to the city. It's because I don't belong here. They can tell. I have no idea how to fix that, no idea how to fit into a place like Richmond. The Fan area, where I live, is full of people who'd stick out like sore thumbs back home in the Shenandoah Valley, with their tattoos and piercings, wild hair and messy beards. Here, I'm the odd woman out.

There's his house, lit up. My heart does a little dance in my rib cage and, for a distracted few seconds, I wonder what that dance would look like in wool. I'd have to build a cavern out of a thicker weave for the rib cage, make puffs for my lungs, figure out exactly what a heart looks like and then somehow create excitement in the mix. Visually, it's a challenge I can't wait to take up.

But not right now. Right now, I'm slowing to a snail's crawl, hoping he's on his porch so I don't actually have to go up to his door and knock.

No luck. The light's on and the porch is empty, except for his beautiful swing and the chair I admire every time I walk by.

Especially if he's sitting in it. Just that thought makes me blush. When he's seated, his thighs look thicker than when he stands, the muscles meatier, his haunches so solid, I swear nothing can break him.

And I'm fantasizing...again.

A shadow appears at his window, startling me. Instead of heading home as I'd planned, I do it. I go up his steps, pull open the screen door and, before I can talk myself out of it, drop the massive knocker twice. I'd do once, but he might think it's a mistake, though that idea's preposterous, given how heavy the thing is. Not like the wind could accidentally set it to knocking and, oh, Lord, I should just go, because I'm a jittery mess. I won't be able to shut up once he opens that door. Surely I'll say something I regret.

I'm about to let the screen go and rush away to hide at home when the door swings open. He's so big, he blocks out almost all the light from inside, though it spills out around his head. Immediately, Squid appears beside him. He woofs, nudges my leg, and goes in after I've given him a little scratch behind the ears.

"Jerusha." Is that a happy voice or an annoyed voice? Impossible to tell with this man.

I swallow, wishing I'd thought to drink a beer before coming over. At least I'd be calmer right now. "Hi."

"Hi," he replies after a few seconds.

"Oh, um. I got pizza and..." Don't tell him about the beer. It's too much. "And I thought you might want to—"

"Who is it?" someone asks from behind him.

After an inordinately long hesitation, he cants his body to one side, giving me a clear view of the beautiful young woman behind him. She's tall and thin and dressed in that perfectly relaxed way girls around here manage—yoga pants and a long-sleeved T-shirt that falls off her bones and boobs like it was made for her. And it was. Her hair's that thick, straight kind that creates a perfectly neat/messy fall from the casual up-do she's clearly got, just for the convenience, not because she's spent hours trying to look like everyone else.

This is the kind of person Karl should be with. Of course it is. Statuesque, hip, casual, at ease in her own skin. Calm and effortlessly gorgeous.

"Oh," I finally manage to pinch out through my tight throat. The woman comes up behind him and slides her hand between his arm and torso. So familiar that she obviously belongs there. "Sorry. Sorry."

"You don't have to—"

"No." I put up a mittened hand, feeling like an absolute fool. Childish clothes, Sesame Street hues, hair that's never met a brush it couldn't destroy. I'm nowhere near this man's league. To think I thought that I could be is ridiculous.

Laughable.

I force a smile, which has to look painful, but I can't help that. It does hurt. More than it should. "You have company. I'm so... I wouldn't... I couldn't... I shouldn't..." *Oh God, shut up. Shut up!* "Thanks! Bye!" I spin to leave and then spin back, nearly colliding with him. "Here. Here, this is... I'm happy to..." Don't say inform you. Don't say it. "I thought maybe you'd..." No. Stop talking! "Art show! Please come!" I shove the invitation at him and take off.

I have no idea how I navigate his steps with my throat in my stomach, much less mine and then my door, with its sticky lock. It doesn't matter that I've had to smash the pizza to do it. I don't have much appetite left anyway.

"Fool. I'm a fool."

You'll never fit in, Papa always told me. He was right. I'll never make it. Never survive. He'd gloat if he saw me right now.

I'd been so proud that I'd not only survived these past months, but managed to thrive in a society that's entirely alien to me. The show, the gallery. Those are a big deal, milestones I'm proud of, but when it comes to this stuff—the social stuff—I've got no idea what I'm doing.

"Foolish, foolish fool." I throw my coat at the hook, uncaring that it slides to the floor, drop the pizza beside it, and lean back against the door. No wonder he left the other night. No wonder he's avoided me since.

And here I canceled the date I'd set up because... I drop my heated face into my still-mittened hands. "Fool."

I feel his footsteps before I hear them. They're heavy on my porch, but silent. The screen door makes its usual creak. When seconds go by without him knocking, I let my hands drop. What is he doing? Is that his breathing on the other side? It's loud, like he's sighed, maybe. Or is talking to himself. I almost laugh. Wouldn't that be hilarious, him muttering on one side, me on the other?

"Um." Another sigh, loud enough this time for me to hear it perfectly. "Jerusha. Are you okay?"

I open my mouth and close it, feeling utterly trapped back here. Caught in emotions that have no place existing. He doesn't want me. It's over.

Okay. As decisively as I can, I nod once. "Karl?" I ask, as if we weren't both just stewing in pseudo-silence on either side of a scarred slab of wood. As if I have *no idea* who could possibly be there. *Well, hello there! What a surprise! Fool,* I mouth. "I'm... I'm fine. I'm sorry."

"Hey. Congratulations on the show. This is huge."

"Oh. Thanks."

"I'll be there. The opening, I mean."

"Great. I'll see you then." Never mind that it's weeks away.

"Could you, uh. Would you mind opening the door, please?"

"Oh. No. No, no, I'm good. You can go back. Go back to your guest. To your..." Girlfriend. I can't bring myself to say it. "You know. I just was—"

"Daughter."

I blink. "Excuse me?"

"My daughter. That was my daughter, Harper."

Ooooooooooooh. What washes over me is such a mixed-up cocktail that I can't begin to describe it. There's relief there, but there's also shame and embarrassment. Curiosity, too, but I can't let that seep out, because there's so much stuff to manage. Or, for want of a better idea, to suppress as best I can.

"Okay."

"Would you open the door?" His voice is soft, low, a little rough. With emotion, like me? Or with laughter, at how ridiculous I've been?

And even that thought's unfair, because, from the moment I first met him, Karl has been nothing but kindness. Never mean, never angry—aside from the other night on my porch. In fact, his interaction with Jed is the only time I've seen him be anything but amiable.

I turn the knob and step back as the door swings in. It's dark in here, which I guess is weird, now that I think about it. He must have guessed that I was on the other side of the door.

I shut my eyes for a mortified three seconds before turning on the lamp. "Hey."

His eyes search mine, drop to scan my body, as if looking for injuries, then land on the pizza box, the coat, the six-pack.

He fiddles with something on the outside of the door. The jingling of my keys sends my humiliation into overdrive. "Here." I don't move when he holds them out to me, so he sets them in their place on my side table. "Might wanna hide those, instead of leaving them right there."

"Sure." I'm nodding, unsure if I can stop. "Okay." We don't worry much about keys where I'm from. I'm not sure Papa even has keys to the house's front door. If he does, they haven't been used in years. The lock probably won't even turn.

"Can we talk for a second?" He's holding my postcard and suddenly I feel silly.

I'm already shaking my head, making a face. "Oh. No. No, we don't need to talk."

"I think we do."

Karl

"You okay?"

"I'm fine." Her smile's about as fake as they come. "You can go back to..." She flaps her mittened hands and I just want to grab them, hold them. Hold her. Doesn't she have any idea how cute she is with all her hair and rainbows and soft-looking yarn?

"Harper."

"Right."

"She took off for yoga or pilates or whatever she does on Thursday nights."

"Okay." She's biting that lower lip again and everything from last week breaks through the dam I'd managed to erect around it —the kiss, the hand-hold, that lip. When she glances up at me from under her unfashionably large eyebrows, I feel just the slightest bit better. Eye contact. One point. "How old is she?"

"Eighteen."

Her "Oh," is almost silent. With a sheepish look, she goes on. "She must think I'm different."

I smile. "You *are* different."

"Great." Her annoyed puff tells me that she's getting over the embarrassed thing. I'm relieved.

"It's a good thing." It's tough to form the right words; partly because I'm not sure what I want to say to her. Despite insisting, I don't really want to talk. If we could move on without acknowl-edging that this happened, I'd be good as gold. But that's the old

Karl talking. The kid who bottled things up, exploded, bottled, exploded. I'd be dead today if I hadn't learned how to communicate. Dammit, being a better man is hard. Worth it, though. I have a whip smart daughter who means the world to me, a father I don't hate anymore, an ex-wife who's healthy and happy—without me. And a neighbor who looks at me like maybe I'm a man she admires. "That beer and pizza just for you? Or you planning to share?"

Her smile smacks into me like a goddamn wave and part of me's proud. Like I earned that look. Like I put it there.

I bend for the box, hand it to her, and grab the six-pack. The way the beers have landed, they'll probably blow when we open them. I follow her down the long, wide hall that's the mirror image of mine, to the kitchen at the far end, waiting for her to turn on lights as she goes. Curiosity has me craning my neck to see the living room and dining room and the spaces beyond. They look almost empty, aside from rugs and cushions and big, funky tapestries on the walls. Everything's colorful and huge. And it smells good. Grassy and fresh. I can never get my house to smell like anything aside from cleaning products or whatever I cooked that day.

The kitchen's the opposite of the other rooms—it's full of stuff. Bright, copper pots and bowls of eggs and seeds. Dried herbs hang from the ceiling, onions and garlic, too.

"This is awesome."

"Really?" Another shy look from those big blue eyes. "Is your place like mine?"

I laugh. "Same floor plan. Well, the opposite. But it's nothing like this." I take in the budget appliances and makeshift work surfaces, modifying my initial reaction. It's appealing because she's filled it with things that seem alive, but underneath it's been cobbled together. "Looking for counters?"

She shrugged, pulling plates out from behind a curtained set of rickety shelves. Someone would need to reinforce those before the weight of the dishes took the whole thing down.

I grab two beers. "You want one?"

At her nod, I lift my chin toward the back door. "Safe to go out there?"

Her curious look makes me smile. "Just need to open these where they won't douse everything." When her expression doesn't change, I explain. "They looked kind of shook up."

"Oh. Right."

Outside, the rickety back stoop complains under my weight. I'm tempted to complain back. Keeping in shape's a lot harder at forty-three than it was at thirty. I manage, but it hurts. Arms outstretched, I pull both tabs. One lets out a spray. The other behaves. I'll give her that one.

I take a long look at her postage stamp of a yard. It's bigger than mine, since I've got my workshop out back. She's landscaped a bit. It's nice. No wonder Squid's always trying to slip through the hole in the fence. I don't blame him.

Back in her glowing kitchen, I accept a plate. "My dog still come over here when I'm working?"

She throws me a shy smile. "Is that okay?"

"You kidding? He loves it here."

"I like him." Something sly passes over her face. "I may have bought treats recently."

I snort. "Yeah, well, don't call me when he decides to move in."

I catch the edge of her adorable smile as she leads the way up the hall to the dining room. She hesitates in the doorway. "Here? Or..." She waves toward the front.

"Living room."

She turns a light on, illuminating the almost empty space. Low table, thick rug, a single ratty armchair, covered in another woven piece.

"Take the chair." She sinks to the floor by the table. I ignore her invitation and join her on the rug, sitting to her right, which puts our bodies perpendicular and our knees close.

After a funny little smile, she eats. And it's something to see. Not ravenous, so much as delighted. It's an event for her, which I like. Prying one piece up, enjoying the stretch of melted cheese, moaning under her breath at the first bite. It's all I can do to eat my own piece without staring. The beer will help. I hold my can up in a toast. She's clearly pleased with that, too, grabbing hers and slamming it against mine too fast and too hard so that it sloshes over both of our hands. I can't help but smile at her giggle. It's catching. I find myself laughing with her in a way I haven't in years.

"Cheers," I say before taking a long pull.

"Oh!" She wipes her first sip off her lips and meets my gaze. "Cheers!" She slaps her can to mine, clearly pleased.

Christ, she's cute. Christ, I shouldn't be here.

And yet, here I am.

I grab my slice, fold it and shove half into my mouth. It's not until I've polished off the first and gone for the second that I notice the way she's watching me.

It's the same way she looked at her pizza before putting it in her mouth.

Everything falls away. I'm hard as nails now, and plagued by guilt. I set my plate down and lean in. "I can't be with you, Jerusha."

She pauses mid-bite, eyes wide. They're so huge, if she even thinks about crying, I'll be able to tell.

"Okay." Something shifts. She finishes the bite and nods. "Would you, um, mind explaining?"

"I'm too old for you."

3

GET OFF

JERUSHA

I fight the desire to look away from his steady gaze. To focus on my plate or my hands or any acceptable location. I was brought up, after all, not to look a man in the eye.

And, goodness, Papa wouldn't approve of this one.

Which is something I've questioned over the last week. Is that what draws me to him? Is it the forbidden thing?

No, I tell myself again. Only this time I can be a million times more certain, because he's right here—in my house, sitting on a rug I made with my own hands, watching me with warm, dark eyes that are more beautiful than anything I've ever seen. No, this isn't about home. This is about me. And him. And the way I feel when he's near.

Too old for me? No, way. "Why?" I force myself to ask.

"Why am I too old?" He looks astonished. "You're, what? Twenty-five?"

"Yes."

"I'm forty-three."

I nod, waiting for more. When nothing comes, I put my plate

down, reach for my beer and take a sip. I like the bubbles—that's not something we had growing up—but I'm not too fond of the bitterness. I'll have to see if I can find one more to my taste.

"So far, you've given me two numbers." I feel my expression shifting into what my family called my know-it-all look, but I honestly can't help it. I know when I'm right. "When's your birthday?"

"It was in January."

"Mine's in March."

He cocks one dark eyebrow. There's a little hole above and below it, as if it's been pierced. I wonder what that feels like, having a needle poke through your skin like that. I'd never felt a needle at all until this year, when I went and got all my vaccinations done after enrolling in grad school. It was a big move for me. I almost laugh. What hasn't been a big move for me? "Okay."

"I'll be twenty-six this year." I give him a smile. "And since you like numbers, here's some math. Forty-three minus twenty-six equals seventeen."

He grins behind his beer and I love that look. It tilts his nostrils up and cuts a dimple into one cheek, so deep I can see it through his beard. The whole look's positively devilish. I want *that*. Whatever's behind that look. Whatever a body and face and brain like that can give me. I don't want the boring Jeds and creepy Scotts and bossy Brians of the world. I don't want any of the guys I've gone out with. I want him.

But does he want me?

Everything inside me sinks to the floor. Of course not. It's not age holding him back. It's that he's not interested. *Fool.* That word floats around again, judgy and mean, but so honest it hurts.

No. Not honest. It's a relic from the past is what it is.

Honesty would be getting all the facts. Honesty would be telling him everything.

Do I have to? A voice whines from the back of my head. I wouldn't be here today if I'd listened to that voice.

"I liked the kiss." The words tumble out. "Did you not like it?"

The smile disappears from his face. He's all dark energy, thrumming so hard I can feel it where our knees touch. Neither of us seems to be breathing.

"I liked it." He sets down his beer. "I just don't think I'm the right person for you."

I give a little nod, though there's nothing acquiescent about it. If he knew me better, he'd get that I'm trying to find another way in.

"Am I the right person for *you*?"

The surprised-sounding laugh he lets out must be involuntary, but he doesn't stifle it. I get the impression he enjoys it when I make him laugh.

"I think you like me as much as I like you."

"Yeah?" Oh, his eyes are glimmering now, something wicked and fierce in their depths. I want to unleash it, to see how that feels.

Keeping my gaze glued to his, I nod.

"What makes you say that?"

"Because you're here."

One massive shoulder lifts in a shrug. "We're neighbors. You're having me over for pizza."

"You sit around eating pizza and drinking beer with your daughter's friends?"

"Hell, no." He shakes his entire body as if the mere thought gives him the willies. "Never." He shoots me a look. "You're sneaky."

"I'm right."

Slowly, carefully, he puts down his beer. "About what?"

"I knew a kiss from you would be amazing."

"Yeah?" His eyes narrow. They're so black, I can't tell the difference between iris and pupil. It doesn't matter. I want to dive in and discover all his dark thoughts.

"Yeah."

"You think about it before the other night?"

I bite my lip and nod.

His gaze lingers on my mouth before sliding back up to my eyes. "What do you want from me, Jerusha of the Valley?"

"I want you to show me everything."

Shock widens his eyes, his pupils blowing up to engulf every bit of warm brown. "You don't even know what that means."

I've never felt excitement like this. Even taking the bus here from the Shenandoah Valley wasn't nearly this...big. I'm breathing hard and fast, feeling wild and fierce.

"No. But I want you to show me."

"Fine." He stands, forcing me to tilt back my head.

For a few wide-eyed seconds, I expect him to pull down his zipper, maybe force himself into my mouth.

I'm so nervous, I can't even tell if I want that or not. How would I respond? There's a curiosity running through me. A dangerous curiosity, my parents called it. And I guess they were right, because this situation is exactly what they'd wanted me to avoid.

Here I am, running headlong at it. Choosing the danger.

It's a relief when he bends for his can and his plate and carries them to the kitchen. I follow slowly, trying to figure out if my brain's functioning correctly or if that even matters when I feel so very alive.

I put the plate in the sink, surprised when he washes it, along with his, and sets it in the rack to dry. I watch a drop of water roll down. Everything's syrupy slow. The way he turns and leans his hips on the counter, the way he watches me, so clearly trying to read me, I almost want to laugh.

And then I do, 'cause if I can't figure myself out, the man's not going to get there.

"What's funny?"

"You. Trying to see into my brain."

"Might help things if I could."

"I'm not so sure of that, actually." I make a face at him. "I'm kind of incomprehensible."

"Okay." He folds arms that are thick as hams across a chest wide as a slab of beef. I'd laugh at my comparisons, but I can't, because I'm suddenly overcome at the image he presents. Forearms sculpted out of muscle and bone, with those short, dark man-hairs I've never gotten the chance to touch, biceps he clearly uses every day, and hands that are big and tough, but also scarred. Someone needs to care for those hands. Someone needs to hold them. "Try to explain it."

I meet his gaze, but have no idea what he's asking for. "Excuse me?"

"Explain what's going on in your head. So I get it."

"Oh. I don't know if I can."

"Try."

4

IN BETWEEN DAYS

KARL

"I told you I'm from the Shenandoah Valley."

"Yeah. Jerusha of the Valley." I smirk. She's so damn cute, with that fluffy cloud of hair framing her face, the big sweater and long skirt that in no way hide the voluptuous body beneath. All of her is an explosion of color—from her clothes to her face, with those blue eyes and auburn brows and brown freckles, pale skin and bright red cheeks.

"Well, you know I'm..." The blush creeps below her high neckline. I brace myself for what she'll say next. "Inexperienced."

I nod, unable to keep my mind from returning to that sweet, short, perfect kiss on her porch the other night. I consider how to respond and come up with nothing. Couldn't get my voice to work right now if I tried.

"I moved here of my own volition. Against my parents' desires." She grimaces. "*Demands*, really."

"Okay."

"They're very religious." This doesn't surprise me. There's something about the way she sits—straight and proper—that says she had an upbringing totally unlike mine. "I grew up praying and reading from the Bible every day. Papa and Mama home-schooled us. We grew what we ate and..." Her hands flutter in an impatient dance. "You get it, right? Papa wasn't...mean. He was strict. Never hurt me, never yelled, though I know I was a trial." Her grin is impish. "I love my parents. And they love me. They just had *no idea* what to do with me. My brothers and sisters are so different. Well, except for Rachel, my little sister. She'd love it here. The others all behaved. Married the right people. Still attend services, you know, have babies and..." She sighs and rolls her eyes. "They don't want to live in the outside world. They love the community, the farms, the Almighty, which I get. I mean, it's nice, right? But..." She shakes her head. "Not for me."

I smile, envisioning her running around, wreaking havoc. Chickens flapping, feathers flying. "Yeah. I can see that."

"You can?" Those lips. That smile. Fuck me, I don't think I've ever been this charmed in my life.

At my nod, she goes on. "Anyway. I tried. I really did. I did everything like I was meant to, only...nothing came out right, you know? I'd cook and nobody could eat it. I'd recite verses as songs. My quilts were not what they were supposed to be and my knit-ting, well—" She indicates the wall behind her, where a massive panel of what looks like yarn is hung. Only it's not knitting the way I've seen it before, it's more like a painting. A landscape, or something, in three dimensions. I stare at it for a few more seconds and suddenly it clears up. Those are mountains, flowing into green, a river. Animals. It looks almost Biblical, now that I see what it is. And it's sort of...heartbreaking. Which doesn't make the least bit of sense.

"It's beautiful."

She snuffles out an embarrassed little laugh. "It's not what they meant when they told me to knit a scarf."

"Damn." I'm shaking my head, laughing, smiling, bright inside in a way I haven't been in forever. "Okay. I get that."

"They love me, you know? I'm just too much. Of everything."

She's not though. She's the perfect amount. Exuberant and bright, but with a deep strain of something serious. Maturity, maybe.

Shit, I hope.

"Anyway. I started making this stuff when I was about thirteen. Got in trouble. Made more. Snuck around making more." She shrugged. "I sold my first piece by accident. My grandmother —she's Mama's mom. Not religious. At all. She hates that my mom married my dad and she... Anyway. She financed me. Everything, from the materials to the laptop to the university education."

"She sent you to school?"

"I moved in with her and did it online. Then..." There's a tightness at the corners of her mouth. I can't tell if she's holding in a smile or an unhappier reaction. "My first piece sold for thirty bucks. The last one I made? Fifteen thousand."

"Holy shit."

"Everything I've sold has been through word of mouth." There's defiance in her expression. It's appealing. "I've got that big art show coming up."

"That's right. At the Werner Gallery." He was impressed. "I'll be at the opening."

She nods and the defiance morphs into something softer. "I sent invitations out to my entire family last week."

"Think they'll come?"

Her half-shrug's incredibly expressive. It tells me that she cares. She wants them to come and thinks they might not. "Guess we'll see."

"They've got to be proud of you."

"I hope so." There's enough hope in her voice to make me angry. What kind of parents wouldn't celebrate their child? Her expression shifts again, from wistful to outright happy. I'm proud of her, even if her family isn't. "Yeah. So, I put money away and, instead of getting married and settling down like my siblings did, I came here. For grad school."

"Interesting choice. You already had an income."

"Yeah. But I *like* school. I love learning. Besides, I wanted a chance at what other kids had. And I figured it would be kind of like an in-between phase for me, you know? Not quite real life. Not quite like being all alone out here. A jumping off pad."

"Makes sense." She's not the innocent I thought she was, she's smart. I feel almost guilty at the assumptions I've made up until now.

"I did some research and decided that VCU was the right place to get my MFA. They've got a good fiber program and—"

"Fiber?"

She rolls her eyeballs toward the wall-hanging.

"Oh, right."

"Anyway. I'm here now." I can feel the long, slow breath she takes. It's almost sensual, like she's sucking in the world, consuming it, experiencing it every way she can. "And I love this city."

"Richmond? Really?"

"Yeah." I want to lick her smile. "It's why I bought this place."

"Dirt town. That's what Harper calls it."

"She doesn't like it here?"

"Says everyone's filthy. Greasy is the word she uses. Figure it's mostly shorthand for tattooed and pierced and artsy." I compress my mouth into a *kid's nowadays* face and then wonder if it's a look she'll even understand. "But, hey, she's spent her whole life here. Sometimes you've gotta leave a place to see the beauty."

I follow her eyes as they make their way back to her art.

"You miss it? The Valley?"

"I miss my family and stuff. But I like it here in Dirt Town," she says with obvious glee. "I love it. Of course, I don't think there's anything wrong with dirt." Her lips fold in on themselves. "I ate mud as a kid."

Impossible not to laugh. "You must've been a lot of fun."

Her face goes serious, eyes narrowing right on me, their focus as solid as a touch. "I still am."

Jerusha

Okay, so I didn't mean to say it that way. I mean, I thought it, but I didn't know he'd see what I was thinking.

Should have, though. I have one of those expressive faces, apparently. Everybody knows what I'm thinking.

"I just mean... I mean... You know. I'm cheerful. And... kind of—"

"Unpredictable."

"Oh." Is that a compliment? My parents didn't see it that way. "What about you?"

He looks taken aback. "What *about* me?"

"I mean. What are you like? Sorry. That doesn't make sense. I mean, what were you like, growing up?"

Karl looks off to the side, reminiscing, maybe. I watch close enough to see his jaw ticking and realize that his expression is anything but placid. "A pain in the ass, mostly. But not like you. Angry."

I cock my head and squint, trying to picture him as a child. I imagine his high cheekbones and wide jaw rounder, his body lanky instead of thick, eyes huge, dark, serious. "When did you get so serious, then?"

His eyebrows lower, all beetled and broody. "Serious? I'm not serious."

"Okay."

"I'm...very..."

I lean forward, hands gripping the counter behind me. How

does he see himself, this big, somber man, whose smiles are so rare. He's smiled five times tonight. Laughed twice. I counted because they're wonderfully hard won.

After a long silence, he shakes his head. "I don't know."

"You're kind."

"No. I'm normal."

"You're a good person. Generous."

"Seriously, Jerusha, don't—"

"My first week here, you fixed my door. And the step. You told me to knock if I ever needed to."

"I'm paranoid."

"Protective."

"I've got a daughter your age."

"Almost a decade my junior."

He growls. "I'd better go. Thanks for—"

"Wait."

This is it. My chance. He's here. He's kissed me. He said he liked it. "I like you, Karl."

"I like you, too, Jerusha."

"I want you to be my first."

Those thick eyebrows almost fly off his head. I'd laugh if everything weren't so twisted up inside.

"Come again?"

"I want you to show me." I swallow, hard, and forge on. "Sex. Show me how to do it."

There's this gap, which one of us is supposed to fill. Him, probably, though I'm the one who created it. I should close it up tight. But I've never been the type of person to do that. I can't fill gaps in conversations and I definitely can't back off once I'm sure of something. And I'm sure of this.

"Do you know how many dates I've gone on in the last six months?" I finally find the words.

Appearing startled, he compresses his lips, shakes his head as if to clear it.

"Guess."

"I don't know. Five?"

"Twenty-seven."

His eyes go wide. "Whoa."

"Twenty. Seven."

"That's a lot."

"Yes, well, I had a lot of time to make up for. But I didn't want a single one of them to kiss me." I raise my hand, palm out, before he says whatever he's about to say.

"I like men. I mean, I'm attracted to them. I know that much. And some of my dates were good-looking, interesting, talented, polite..." *But none of them were you.* "But none of them are what I'm looking for."

He narrows his eyes. "You think I am?"

"I like how you kiss." It's all I can offer right now, when he's giving me nothing—not an inkling of what's on his mind shows in that scowl. Well, probably annoyance, but nothing beyond that.

It hurts, I admit, how much that kiss gave me, how much I felt from those few, perfect seconds, when he clearly felt nothing.

"The kiss was..." He blinks a few times, breathes out, once, and shakes his head, as if searching for words. Finally, when his gaze lands on me, I know he's not kidding. "Just not your guy. Okay?"

I smile, so hard my cheeks hurt. "Yes. Yes, of course. Okay."

"Thanks for uh, the pizza. And beer."

"You're welcome." If I stay like this, I'll crack. But if I stop smiling, he'll see how much this means to me and I can't have that. "My pleasure."

"All right." He reaches back to rub his nape with one thick hand. It's an uncomfortable-looking motion that I've never seen him do. A quick look around, landing on me for three seconds, before he walks back up the hall to the front door. "Night."

"Night-night." My grin's still fixed, probably diabolical and creepy, like one of those plastic dolls with the smile painted on. I'll bet my teeth are nothing but a slash of white.

That's how I feel, as he carefully closes the door, like a bunch of moving parts that don't belong. Like a too-big, too-weird, mash-up: half dowdy Barbie and half Little Orphan Annie, with her fat halo of frizzy hair and bright-colored dress.

Old Maid Barbie. Except it's not the spinster part that bugs me—I don't want to get married. I don't want kids and diapers and skinned knees and advice. I like how things are. I'm free and alone, in my long, skinny row house in Richmond's Fan district, with my scowling next-door neighbor. I'd had hopes, but...

Never mind. I'm fine with my life as it is.

I mean, I wouldn't mind having sex at some point. The way people do. With orgasms and dirty talk and pure, unadulterated lust.

Now, I guess I'll have to find someone else to do it with.

Back to the dating board.

5

COME OUT AND PLAY

KARL

"What the hell's gotten up your butt?" Harper sidles up to the bar and sets down her empty tray, planting her hands on her hips like the bossy little woman she is. Or will be. Christ I don't know anymore.

I give her a look. "Nothing."

"It's not nothing, Dad."

"I'm always ornery."

She snickers. "True words, father dearest. But this..." She sweeps me with eyes that are mine, on steroids—bigger, brighter, with thick lashes, and goopy mascara that I can't get her to stop slopping on. Not that I insist. I've discovered that telling her what I think almost never works. She hasn't gotten any ink yet, and, given how much I had by her age, I count that as a major win. "This is some new level brooding."

"I'm fine." I slap my hand lightly on the bar—back to business. "What you need?"

"Two Coronas and a G & T, please, Pops."

Rolling my eyes at the nickname, I grab the beers from the

cooler and come back to pour the drink, ignoring the way my daughter squints at me, giving me the full-on Harper McCoy X-ray vision treatment. If I'm not careful, she'll figure out exactly what's bothering me and then—

"I know." Chewing on the end of her pen, she smiles, lifting one eyebrow in a look I passed down, but she's perfected. "It's cute lil neighbor girl, isn't it?"

I drop the drink on her tray and walk away, ignoring her whooping.

Because dammit, she's right.

Ever since I left Jerusha's place last week, I've been a mess. Not a fall-down-drunk mess, the way I was when I was younger, but the kind of mess that waits up late to make sure his young neighbor doesn't get mauled on her porch by another date. The kind of mess who spends more time at his front window than he ever has before. The kind who searches for Jerusha Graff on the internet and almost has a heart attack at the prices her artwork brings in. And, Jesus, yeah, a mess who jerks off in his bed at night, imagining it's those busy little hands of hers and that pert mouth instead of his own callused fist.

The door opens. "Hey, sailor." I turn as my business partner, Dave, walks into the restaurant. "How's tricks?"

Rather than respond—'cause what kind of answer does he honestly expect to such a pointless question?—I nod.

"Shit, man. Not even a 'Hey, Dave?' Things that bad?"

"Good."

"Dinner?"

"Booked up."

"Damn. Wanted a table." *Should've reserved, you privileged prick.* He sits on a stool and turns to survey the crowd. Which is good, especially given that it's a Tuesday. In fact, business has been incredible. No thanks to Dave. "We'll eat at the bar."

I raise an eyebrow in his direction. "Using the royal We now?"

"Got a date." He smirks. "Young, cute, nerdy. Gagging for it. I'm getting laid tonight."

I can't look at his fucking face for another second. I turn to the beer cooler and pause. "Your usual or are you trying to impress?"

"Nah. Not this girl." His grin's frankly disgusting. "This girl's geeky. Hungry for cock. Won't care what I drink."

With a disgusted sound—lost on him, of course—I ignore his outstretched hand and put his Bud on the bar.

"Give me a tequila, too. Double."

Christ, I can't wait till I've bought him out completely. In six months, the place is all mine. I've built what was once Richmond's sleaziest sports bar—known for back alley quickies and coke in the walk-in—into the city's hippest, most sought-after restaurant. I make my own fucking cocktail shrubs, for God's sake.

This asshole's the reason I fought so hard to keep Harper from working here. Until I realized that at least here I could keep an eye on her in my bar. Since the talk, during which I let Dave know that if he so much as looked at my daughter, I'd rip his testicles off and shove them down his throat, things have been okay.

He's a nasty, entitled, grown-up frat boy, whose daddy's money is the only thing that's kept him out of prison. I wouldn't wish him on anyone—much less some unsuspecting young woman.

Harper calls from the end of the bar and I go fill a couple orders, happy to see that the rosemary-jalapeño margaritas are selling. Our reputation's grown over the past year and I'm proud. This business is my retirement and my daughter's legacy. And, yeah, I'd like to get out from behind the bar more and into the workshop, where I work with wood and metal instead of booze, but I like the place. One day, the dream is to let it run itself and devote all my time to the other stuff. I'm getting there, a step at a time.

Until then, I let myself enjoy the thrum of a well-run restaurant. The dinner rush takes over, its ebb and flow of people and orders making time speed by. I like mixing drinks. I like chatting with customers. I really like the feel of being back here, watching over everything, with a finger on the pulse of the place.

The door opens, letting in a whoosh of cold air. I glance over to see if the hostess is available to greet the person, and go still.

Even without seeing her face, I know it's Jerusha—all wild hair and wild energy. I like that energy. It speaks to me, even from across the room. And I swear she can feel my stare. She looks up, catches my eye, and goes completely still. It's out of character, given how much movement goes on in that little body.

The smile that takes over her face isn't just flattering, it's life-giving. Like every on-edge second I've lived this past week melts away and I feel—

"Jerusha?" I blink at Dave's over-loud voice, blasting through the crowd's easy hum.

"Uh. Yes. Hello." Her eyes cut back to me before landing on him.

"Well, *hey there*, cutie." He actually fucking winks. My blood pressure skyrockets.

"Oh." After flicking her eyes my way again, she walks up to the bar, all bouncing curls and floor-length skirt, and a huge, multicolored poncho, and puts out a mittened hand. "You're Dave?" Her smile's a little hesitant, but still so lovely, I can almost taste it. I *have* tasted it. Something low and feral rears its ugly head—a part of me that hasn't seen the light of day in decades. I shove it down. Bad things happen when I let it out.

"That's me." He gets off the barstool and bypasses her handshake, going straight for an overly tight hug that she clearly isn't prepared for. When our eyes meet over his shoulder, I can't help but widen mine with a completely unnecessary—and unfair —*what are you doing here?* expression.

She extricates herself from Dave's grasp and steps back,

eyeing the other barstools before sliding into the one that Dave pats for her.

When Dave glances my way, I give him a look designed to remind him of past conversations. I swear, if he so much as touches her...

Harper chooses that moment to sashay over to the bar with a bunch of empties. "Ho-ly crappers," she says with obvious glee. "Is that your cute neigh—"

"Yes," I bite out as I bus her bottles and throw them into the recycling bucket way too hard. "What you need?"

She reaches for a bowl of peanuts I keep on the ledge behind the bar and pops a handful into her mouth. "Not a thing. This..." She waves a hand toward Dave, who's leaning too close to Jerusha, then points at me. My eyes go narrow and hard. "This is all I need. Way better than the housewives."

"You got an order?"

"Oh. Three house reds."

I pour them and watch Harper sashay over there to chat with Jerusha, handling Dave with an aplomb that belies her eighteen years. She's slippery, my daughter.

A minute later, she returns to grab her drinks with a sly smile. "Jerusha had no idea this place was yours."

Of course not. I'd never told her.

Harper leans closer, losing her usual smirk. "She needs to get out of that situation. Right. Now."

My fists tighten automatically. Harper's right. She does.

Frustration makes me antsy, with a side of simmering rage. If I were ten years younger, I'd serve myself a double bourbon in a mug and stew. But I'm not that asshole anymore.

Instead, I drink soda water...and stew.

"The lady wants a white," Dave calls a minute later.

Inhaling deeply, I amble over to the pair and force an amiable expression onto my face—not easy when I want to grab Dave by the scruff and haul him out of his own bar. "Jerusha."

"Hi Karl."

"You, uh, know Dave?"

"Oh!" Her eyelashes flutter, which Dave will probably take for flirtation. I'm guessing it's nerves. And not the good kind. "Um. No. No, we just met."

"You know my date?" Dave turns to me, while surreptitiously sliding a hand down her back, so far it's gotta be hitting her ass.

She shifts forward, clearly uncomfortable.

"Dave," I growl.

He turns and catches my eye, looking clueless. I'm guessing my expression must convey at least part of what I'm feeling because he pulls his arm away, fast. Good.

When she throws me a smile, I swear my central nervous system takes a hit.

Part of my vision goes black, which is exactly how I'd react if he laid a hand on my daughter. Or anyone I care about.

No. No way is Dave fucking Green going to be this woman's first *anything*. He's the absolute definition of a prick; the kind of guy who pushes and wheedles and gets away with as much as he can. I've heard the stories—mostly straight from his mouth—and he's never met a woman he didn't want to treat like shit.

When I don't answer within an acceptable time limit, Jerusha clears her throat. "We're neighbors."

I give a quick nod and walk away to refill a wine.

Harper comes back with another order. While I make her cocktails, she meanders back over to the pair at my bar. A look passes between the women and I wonder if Harper's somehow expressed how inadvisable Dave is.

Even so, she doesn't leave. He's moved his stool closer. Harper comes back to me, all business.

"You need to do something, Dad."

"Do something?"

"Don't play dumb, Pops. Even Mom says you're one of the smartest people she knows—and she hates your guts."

"She's here of her own free will, Harper. What do you want me to—"

"She asked you out, didn't she? Before this."

I open my mouth to deny it and then think better of it. Harper's super power is seeing through my lies.

"What? And you told her you're too old or some Boomer crap like—"

"I'm not a Boomer, Harper." Which she knows very well.

"So, you're saying you're okay with—"

My eyes focus down the bar, where something's happening. Dave's standing up, looking at a wet spot on his lap. Jerusha's glass is empty.

Oh, shit.

He yells something, which I can't hear through the rushing in my ears. And that's a good thing, because whatever he has to say, it's better if I don't hear it.

And then the dam bursts.

So full of adrenaline that I can't feel my fingers, I leave the bar and stalk over to where she's sitting, eyes on fire, color high. Whatever the fucker did to her, he'll regret it.

"You okay?"

"Yes." Her lips are tight, the skin around them white. "But he tried to put his hand on my... My..." She waves a hand around her thigh.

"Little bitch threw her wine at—"

I lose it completely. Dave weighs nothing when I grab him by the collar and drag him behind me, ignoring his protests, barely registering his hands clawing at mine.

To the front door and outside, where I throw him to the sidewalk and watch him land like a side of meat.

It's clear he sees—or feels—that I'm not the amiable guy he's dealt with up until now, because when I squat and get *right* in his face, he shrinks back, uncharacteristically silent. Scared.

"You never set foot here again."

"I'm still part owner, you can—"

"I'll call my lawyer, make the a final payment soon as I can. Buy you out early." I've got no idea where I'll find the cash, but I will. I'll sell a goddamn kidney if it means never seeing this bastard again. "Go."

He scuttles back on all fours like a crab and lurches up, then takes off down the street at a quick clip. I hope it's the last I ever see of the prick.

Without another word, I turn. She's there, in the open door, wide-eyed.

I walk up to her, hating that she's seen my inner monster, but maybe relieved that she no longer thinks I'm the right guy for the job.

"You still want me to...show you?" Fuck, I sound rough, out of control.

Her tongue flicks out to lick her lower lip. She nods.

"Fine." I bend down, tangle my fingers in the hair at her nape, and press my forehead to hers, imprinting myself on her, though I'm the one who'll come out of this burned. She snares my gaze and doesn't let it go, proving how firmly I'm already hooked. "I'll do it."

6

MYSTERIOUS WAYS

JERUSHA

Everyone stares when I get back inside, but I'm not bothered by that. I'm feverish from the contact with Karl. I'm angry and excited, full of emotion. Alive.

I meet Karl's eyes.

Adrenaline—or is it fury?—looks good on this man, like he was born in another era, one where men swung sledgehammers to settle disputes, and came home painted in blood, smeared in dirt.

I'm not the violent sort, but something's happening between my legs right now and I can't deny the pull.

I grab my bag and take out my wallet to pay for the wine—not even a little regretful at where it ended up.

"What do I ow—"

"Nothing. As my Nana used to say, '*Put that purse away*'"

"What accent is that supposed to be?"

"Oirish." My only response is to raise my brows. "That bad, hm?" He shakes his head and, though he's not smiling, there's an unmistakable light in his eyes. It's possible I put it there. "Let me buy you dinner."

"Oh, you don't have to do that."

"I want to do that, Jerusha. It's the least I can do after how that asshole took advantage."

"Yeah, but you didn't—"

"Let me."

"Okay." I offer a smile, suddenly worried that giving in to me wasn't what he actually wanted. Had he offered as a way to keep me out of trouble? No way would I accept that.

"Listen." I plant my hands on the bar and stand on the rungs of the stool to stretch closer to him. "Don't feel obligated, okay? To show me the ropes? It was just an off-the-wall idea the other day, and—"

"Nope. Too late now." He blinks the demons from his eyes. "Unless you change your mind, obviously."

When I nod and sit back down, he follows, like there's a two-foot cord stretched between us. "Did you?"

"What?"

"Change your mind?"

"Are you kidding me? I've wanted to kiss you since the moment I..." I shut my eyes and fight a losing battle against a hot blush. No point fighting it. No point denying it. I open my eyes and force them to meet his. "I've thought about this. A lot. With *you.*"

"Me, too."

"Really?"

"You surprised?"

"I didn't...I mean, I sort of thought... You're doing me a favor here."

"You're..." He shuts his eyes, shaking his head for a few seconds before looking at me again. "The feeling's mutual, Jerusha."

"You like me," I say, unable to keep the wonder from my voice.

"Yeah." When he nods, I imagine there's a touch of that same thing there—a sort of happy surprise. Like we've been unexpectedly blessed. Giving me a warm look, he pours a glass of wine and slides it in front of me. "Anything you don't like?"

My eyes go wide. Is he really trying to talk about this here? "Well, I mean, the only thing I've ever done was when you kissed me the other night. But I liked that."

"Okay," he says, with an odd expression. "Is there any *food*, though, that you don't care to eat? Or allergies or anything?"

"Oh, goodness." I hide my burning face behind both hands. "That wasn't... Oh, geez. Okay." I shake my head. "No. Nope, I eat everything."

"So, raw squid and calf liver and..." Suddenly his voice lowers to a whisper and he's right there in front of me. "Hey." I open my eyes to find him smiling warmly. "You okay?"

"Embarrassed is all."

His head tilts to one side, eyes glowing darkly. "You're so damn...cute."

"Really?"

"Shit." He takes a quick look around, looking like he just woke up to where he is. "Be right back." He folds his lips together and disappears through a door to what must be the kitchen.

The second he's out of sight, Harper—Karl's beautiful daughter—skips over. "I'm seeing things, right?"

"Seeing things?" I'm so hot, I must look like I've been boiled in water.

"My dad's into you."

"Oh, no, he's just... I mean, I..." What am I doing? I can't tell his daughter that I asked him to show me what a good kiss is like. "I...I'm..."

"Hey. Hey. Wait a sec. This is amazing." She nudges me with one slender shoulder. "I've literally *never* seen him into anyone.

He's a monk. Fricking Friar Karl, self-flagellating at home 'cause he was a wild man in his youth and sowed one too many wild—" She cuts off abruptly as the door from the back swings open, revealing her father with his arms full. After a quick elbow nudge and a wink, she disappears into the crowd of diners, humming.

"What'd Harper tell you?"

"I...I think I'm not supposed to tell you." It's not like this type of thing's happened to me before.

He plunks down silverware and a napkin, along with a basket of Heavenly-scented bread and a ramekin of butter. They send my tastebuds into overdrive.

A distrustful squint takes over his face. "Why not?"

"She was nice. I don't want to..." I wave my hand, as if that's any sort of explanation.

"Nice?" He harrumphs "That's good enough for me, I guess."

I eye the bread. "That smells amazing."

"Have some."

"Oh, no, I'll wait."

"Do it, Jerusha. Eat the bread."

"Yeah? I'm not supposed to, you know, wait until the food arrives, or something?"

"No." He breaks open a roll, releasing steam and enough scent to set off a rabid growl in my belly. "Whoa. Hang on." In a hurry now, he spreads butter on the bread, and hands it over. "Dig in."

I do. And it's so good, I moan.

I barely take notice when Karl blows out a hard breath, slaps the bar, and walks away.

I swallow the bread and stuff another bite into my mouth.

A couple minutes later, he's back with a small terra cotta plate of shrimp in a chunky sauce. "Spiced camarones," he says.

When I don't immediately respond, he indicates the dish with his chin. "Go on. Tell me what you think."

I pick up a shrimp and bite into it and holy mother, it's the best thing I've ever tasted. I don't say a word, but he must know I love it, because his eyes are on me and he's nodding a little, like he knows.

He pushes the basket of bread closer. "Dip it in the sauce."

It's sweet and salty and hot, hot, hot, with garlic and spices I've only recently discovered. I swear I'm drooling when I say, "That. Is the best. Thing. I've ever eaten. Hands down."

He grins. "Just wait."

The second shrimp goes down the same way, although I notice different things this time—a perfumey green herb that lifts the whole dish up. I love it.

"I want to marry this." I'm half laughing, half moaning and he joins in, though he hasn't even tasted it. "Here." I push it toward him. "Eat some."

"Nope. Just enjoying the show."

"Hey!" I say, halfheartedly. I can't be bothered to feel embarrassment. I know how I am about food. I know how it looks, and I don't care. The fact that he appreciates it makes me like him that much more. I really do like him. I like his restaurant, too, and his daughter.

My eyes follow his progress down the bar, to where two men have sat down for dinner. He shakes their hands and chats with them, looking friendly and warm and happy to see them. It's probably wrong to objectify him, but it's hard not to from this distance. There's something so confident about the man. Tall and straight and hefty in a way that excites me. I imagine all that power doing things to me, though I still don't know exactly what it is that I want.

I mean, I've watched sexy stuff. I've seen what people do. My parents insisted that curiosity was one of my worst vices. I know at least some of what two bodies can do together, to each other. But *that man* over there—standing so straight and strong, so confident and warm—I've *tasted* him. I've felt his firm touch. I know how he smells, close up. Knowing and experiencing aren't even in the same realm.

My eyes drink him in now as he pours a few things into a big, silver cup, shakes it all up carefully serves it to his two new customers. He's rolled up his sleeves to just below his elbows—a place I've never admired on a human before—which showcases tattoos I had no idea were there, muscles, and thick-knuckled fingers that work with absolute ease and expertise. Will he work me like that?

I'm breathing hard just thinking about it. It doesn't occur to me that I'm staring until his gaze shifts to mine. Just that eye to eye contact rearranges my insides.

A shiver runs through me. He knows what I'm thinking. He knows.

He pushes off the bar, saying something to his customers, without taking his eyes off me. Peripherally, I notice them watching me, probably wondering what's gotten into Karl McCoy.

Slowly, he prowls toward me, an inexplicable dichotomy of tight muscles and loose limbs. How would it feel to let that capable body take over? No. Not would, I realize with a startled little jolt. Will. How will that feel?

"Got a minute?" he asks, which I don't immediately understand.

"Um, sure."

"Follow me," he growls before heading through a wooden door in the back of the room.

Karl

I shouldn't be doing this. Not here, where I've literally fired employees for inappropriate behavior. I shouldn't be doing this, but I am.

And she's following me, which... Hell, I don't know if I'm pleased or unhappy about that.

Bullshit.

I glance down to where my cock's pressing against the front of my jeans. Calling bullshit on myself's sort of been my mantra for my forties. So, yeah, I'm excited as hell that she's right behind me.

I unlock my office door, wait for Jerusha to step inside, and follow her in, locking it behind me.

"I, uh..." Shit. What an asshole. Full restaurant out front, and I'm back here, stammering in front of the woman who wants me to show her the ropes. "Come here."

She's in my arms in under two seconds flat and I remember, Christ, I *remember*, how good she felt.

Only the kiss is better tonight, frantic and heated, like we've been plopped down in the middle of this attraction, instead of starting in the very beginning like the other night.

And, goddamn, the middle is one hell of an inferno. She's wrapped around me, stroking, feeling, consuming me—arms, shoulders, neck—like she's been thinking about doing this and she's *finally* got the chance.

Which is precisely how I feel. There's no measuring or careful weighing here, no learning or getting to know each other —this shit is fire. And I'm jumping in headfirst. Lips, teeth, tongue, and every one of my senses.

My hand's in her hair, holding her tight, tighter. So tight, she stumbles back to land against the door. She deepens the kiss and those moans—the ones I couldn't get enough of at the bar—are back, only they're hungrier. Shit, that hadn't seemed possible.

I yank myself back, with difficulty. "Like this?"

She nods, wraps her hand around my neck and pulls me back in and, fuck, I've got to feel her, taste her, smell her down there. One fist's got her pegged to the door, the other slides over her thin sweater, feeling warm, curvy flesh beneath.

I slip under the sweater to find soft skin, grunt at the heat, and stroke down to where her rounded hip's the perfect size and give. Another pained sound tears from my throat. My hips tilt forward until my cock's against her. Dammit. This isn't right.

I rip myself away from her plush, hungry mouth and hover there, breathing her air, her smell, her high whimpers.

"Shit, Jerusha." I glide my mouth over the side of her face to her ear and whisper, "You're killing me."

"S'it okay? Am I doing it right?"

What?

I loosen my hold on her hip, breathe, and pull away. Just a little, 'cause, shit, I'm not ready to put space between us yet.

"I'm on fire."

I don't hear her laugh as much as I feel it—a vibration from her chest to mine. "Good." Her lips curve up, puffy and pink and more sensual than anything I've touched before.

She tilts her hips forward to meet mine again. Air escapes me. "Watch out." I whisper, meeting her playful gaze. "I'm an old man. Been a while since I had this much excitement."

She lets out a teasing giggle. "You just picked up a guy and threw him out on the sidewalk."

I plant a firm kiss on her lips, drinking in the unfamiliar taste of her—just one more for the road. "I could do that in my sleep. This..." I step back and indicate the space between us. "This is rare." I don't tell her it's not just the actions I mean, it's the sensation. Not just the newness of her, but the... Shit, I've got to tell her. I'm done keeping shit back. "We've got...chemistry, you and I. That's what I mean. Not just that we're kissing. It's that we're kissing and the whole fucking world could explode and I couldn't care less."

She huffs out a sound. "Thought it was just me."

Our gazes meet and hold, like they're meant to, and I spend the next few seconds in my head, because frankly, this shit's scary. I've been married, dammit. I've been in love. It's just never been like this. Incendiary. I worry about her. I worry about myself.

But not enough to stop this.

I'm not an idiot.

With a smile, I tuck her hair behind her ear and give her enough space to finally move. "Better get back. Make sure the restaurant hasn't blown up."

The look she throws me is decidedly flirtatious. If I didn't know better, I'd say the woman knows exactly what she's doing. "They probably called the fire department on *us*," she says and it's so goofy, so unexpected—this whole damn thing—that I laugh, the sound trailing off as I throw my arms around her and give her a happy hug. I kiss the top of her head and put her away from me.

"Let's go see if your second course is ready."

7

BLISTER IN THE SUN

JERUSHA

Magic. Pure magic. The night, the food—dishes and dishes, tastes and flavors like I've never experienced. Steak and sweet potatoes and roasted mushrooms, green bean French fries, hot fiery slaw and a bright, tangy salad that almost made me weep. Every dish I tried had him going back into the kitchen for more, as if my reactions fed him as much as the food fed me. Then there was the wine. Three glasses, making me happy and silly and light.

I'd have swapped every bit of it for more of that kiss in the back room.

I swipe a hand over my mouth, sad that his taste's gone, but still so happy, I can't help but smile.

I want to run all the way home...and then I do. There's no one around to tell me not to. No disapproving frowns or angry glares. Just a few dog walkers, maybe some diners returning home, bellies full. There are rows upon rows of long skinny houses, lined up side to side, similar, but different, even from the street. From dilapidated to sparkling, drab to rainbow-bright. I love this place. Pumpkins on stoops, piles of rustling leaves, begging to be messed up, and wood smoke, which reminds of home.

I slow about a block from my house, breathing hard, lungs aching from the cold—but even that feels good. A fitting end to a wondrous night. Some houses are lit up, windows bare enough to see inside, but they're like mine, which means only the entry and front room are visible, the rest are a mystery.

He's like that—Karl. A certain way on the surface—brusque and gruff. Tough and a little mean. It's what he shows the world, what he wants most people to see. But behind the bar, another side came out. His regular customers got a man of hospitality and kindness. Mellow, warm. I imagine his daughter sees him that way.

He showed me more, though, tonight. The white blaze at the heart of him, a brilliant core, so hot that it burned.

I'm breathing hard at the memory now, rather than from my run, like I've sprinted a marathon instead of five blocks. I'm on fire—from him.

And I like it.

I get home, brush my teeth, and get undressed, all jittery and excited, and flop onto my cool blankets, naked. Goose bumps race over my skin. I'm sensitive and cold on the surface, while my insides roil like lava. Still not entirely comfortable with my own touch, I reach down, tentative and a little ashamed, to caress the place between my legs.

My mons, it's called here—the plump curl-covered mound that I used to press soap to in the bath as a teen. Shame. That's what I'd felt back then as I'd scrubbed hard in search of sensation.

No more, I insist, again. And again, and again. No more shame, no more fear of a God who'd rather hurt than celebrate. No more living for the promise of a brighter afterlife.

In the moment, I throw off what I've been taught and dive into what I've learned on my own.

My hair down there is beautiful. It's wiry and thick—luxurious. I don't have to move lower to feel the wetness—also a sort of luxury. Natural, and God-given, if I'm to believe He created me.

But I don't. I can't. It's not who I am. Instead, I pull away from dogma and dig into warm, pliant flesh—slick and swollen from desire. My labia—lips. Sensitive and lush. Complex in a way that mirrors my insides, though somehow simple once I got to know them.

My finger grazes the miraculous seat of all my pleasure, pushing air from my lungs in a silent gasp. My clitoris. Clit. The seed of pure sin. Would this spot even exist if we were made as my parents claim? No. I let myself moan aloud, give my bliss sound and space in a world that wanted to deny it. And then, because I've truly given in to my flesh's needs, I slide down, to my opening, circle it and ease one finger inside my slick, hot hole.

Until I came here, I was ignorant of my own anatomy. Now, I know the name for this, too, and everything inside. How babies are made—and orgasms. I smile. *That* is an art I've perfected in a very short time.

I could do it now in under a minute, but I've learned that true extravagance lies in making it last.

He appears again, behind my eyelids, only it's not looks I'm seeing now, it's the other things he gave me tonight. From the press of his hips to mine, I got a taste of what is contained in those muscles. Not just good to look at or to touch, they're full of power. What would that feel like, unleashed?

A shiver runs through me and the orgasm's edging up, despite the lack of friction. A car thrums outside and I hold my breath. Is it him? Already home? The engine ebbs. Not him. I'm disappointed, but also excited. Anticipation is sweet when there's something to look forward to.

I think back on the way the evening ended, with Karl walking me out onto the wide sidewalk. "You walking home?" he asked.

I nodded. "Don't have a car."

"You drive?"

"Farm vehicles."

He grinned. "Got a license?"

"Working on it."

"Want me to run you home?"

"No. I'm fine."

His face wrinkled into that scowl that hides so much and reveals even more. "It's late."

"I always walk."

He harrumphed, a low grumpy sound that appeals to me on a level I need to further explore.

Right now, on my bed, just thinking about that sound sends my nerves rushing higher. Unable to hold back, I sink two stiff fingers into my wet vagina, and grunt at the stretch. It'll be him, one day. If he takes it this far.

He will. He has to. It has to be him with those hard eyes, hard muscles, the hard erection he pressed to me tonight. I gasp at each penetration, feeling empty and achy, wetter than I've ever felt myself, smelling of musk and my own desire.

What does his smell like?

I shut my eyes hard at the question. It's too much, too real and animal. It sends my other hand down to rub messily at my clit. There's no talent in my right hand, no rhythm, which makes the whole thing right and wrong, at once. Like maybe it's his hand getting a feel for me, instead of my own. Like maybe he'd rub me here if I asked him to.

In my mind, I see the glint of silver in short dark hair, the clasp of his rough hand on my waist and hip, which only my imagination can provide. And right now, it tells me that he'd squeeze harder—not to hurt me, but because he couldn't help it.

Or maybe, I don't know, maybe he's controlling himself, and me. Maybe he's holding me still to make me take the pleasure. Maybe he's so in charge that he restrains me and forces it onto me.

Before the next awkward stroke's finished, I'm climaxing,

higher, stronger than I have before. It startles me like a slap across the face, leaves me hollowed out. I'm not myself for the next handful of seconds. Or if I'm me, I'm a version I've never experienced before. Elemental. Stripped down. Blank as a newborn.

All body. No mind. No shame. Nothing but flesh and pulse and satisfaction.

It takes a while to come down, to re-emerge, not so much from my orgasm as from a chrysalis.

Sex with Karl won't turn me into a new woman any more than leaving the Valley did. But given how much I've gotten from this single masturbation session, I suspect it'll strip away another veil; another piece of my parents' armor.

On the heels of that thought comes the realization that this carapace they've forced on me, my entire life was, indeed, for my own good, as they insisted. They force-fed me scripture not to hurt me or to quell my true self, but to protect me. From the world.

In the next breath, I'm half laughing, half crying, so full of tenderness for the people who raised me that nothing could hold it in.

Silly, silly parents. Don't they realize there's no saving me from myself?

8

HOW DO YOU WANT IT?

KARL

"Too old for this shit," I mutter as I pull the back door closed and head to my truck for the quick drive home. I mean closing up after a long shift on my feet, but Jerusha comes to mind, too.

Not that she's been far off at any point tonight.

My brain's on a goddamn seesaw of memories versus good intentions.

Am I really the guy for the job? is the question I keep coming back to.

Compared to Dave fucking Green, the answer's yeah. But there's got to be someone her age who'll treat her well and show her the ropes. Someone compatible in a way I could never be.

Then that kiss comes back and compatible's blown out of the water. What I experienced with her in those few stolen minutes is—*shit*—I shiver at the memory. Not even the same realm as compatibility. Caitlin and I were compatible. And look where that ended up—arguments and anger and shitty divorce, with Harper in the middle.

When I touch Jerusha, it's like fresh connections are made in my brain. Like dead neurons firing up, like... Shit. Like a new lease on life.

Who'll be teaching who? I wonder, as I pull into the alley behind my house and park tight against the back fence. I glance up at her place—as I do every time I come home—and see a light on. I've never been upstairs, so I have no idea if that's her room or someone else's, but I'm dying to see her again. To test this newfound feeling.

Though I'm dead on my feet, I pull out my phone and fire off a quick text.

Waiting up?

Couldn't sleep. :-) Too excited.

Dammit. I'm about to do something stupid.

Want company?

Only if it's yours.

Squid okay, too?

Of course.

Be about five minutes—back door.

I ignore the voice telling me to slow this down, grab Squid from my place and give him a quick walk around the alley.

I take her steps two at a time, arrive at the back door as she opens it and scoop her in to my body. Squid slides by—probably to investigate the rest of the house. I honestly have no clue where he goes, because I notice what she's wearing and go brain-dead. Nothing but a threadbare T-shirt that ends just past her ass with a faded cross over the heart. As if I needed convincing that I'm a lecherous old man.

"This T-shirt..." I pull at the hem.

"I know. It's old and ugly." She plucks it from my fingers. "Didn't have time to change."

"It's... fucking *divine*." I'm laughing as the words come out, punctuating my dive straight to hell, in the arms of this young woman.

"Come here." I slide cold hands beneath the thin fabric, run them up, and stutter to a halt when there's nothing there but smooth skin. My whispered *"Fuck,"* is reverent. It's the way I felt as a kid the first time I opened one of my big sister's Victoria's Secret catalogues. My cock comes alive, angels sing, and I swear I'd die a happy man right now.

"Didn't have time to put on underwear."

Yes you did, I'd say, if I could talk, though it's presumptuous and maybe a little too forward. Too forward? Christ, I'm a mess of contradictions.

All I manage is a long, low, *Oh*. It's heartfelt, though. She has to know that I like it.

"Nobody's ever..." She shivers, pressing her soft breasts to my chest. "Touched me there before."

My cock's pounding in my jeans. At this point, she'll touch me and I'll come. Which is what happens when teenagers first start messing around. It's not what happens to forty-three-year-old men.

I plant my hands at her waist—*over* the cotton tee—and push her a foot away from me.

"First lesson..." I decide, on the fly, "...is dirty talk." It'll keep me from making a fool of myself.

Her brows go up, her lips slowly follow. "There's a syllabus?"

Air huffs painfully from my lungs in an approximation of a laugh. "Making it up as I go." I nod, firm in my decision. "But dirty talk's a good first step."

"I'm all ears." Her grin's enormous, so typical of this woman. Joyous and honest and real. It slays me.

"If we're going to do this right." *And we are.* "We have to take it slow, make it good for you. The way it should be." No more frantic dry humping against restaurant doors. And if I come in my pants, so be it.

"Want a drink?"

"Water would be good."

I follow her progress to the cupboard, my eyes glued to her

face until I remember that I'm allowed to stare at those plump, strong thighs. Just looking satisfies a thirst I've denied myself these past few months.

"Know how you said you've wanted to..." She reaches high, revealing just the hint of those two half-moon curves and I can't speak past the sudden dryness in my throat.

When she looks at me there's expectation, but not an ounce of awareness of what's happening inside me. This woman has no idea what she does to me. None.

"Crushing on you hard, Jerusha."

Though her features don't move, they change—become brighter, maybe. "Yeah?"

I nod, slow and in control. "You got any idea how gorgeous that ass is?"

Her jaw drops. "Is it?"

"I could tell, you know, that I'd like your body." I step closer. "I just didn't know how much."

"Oh." Her eyes slide down my front, to the floor, then back up. Acquiring somewhere along the way, a dirty little glint. "I think about you without clothes on all the time."

Good thing she hasn't filled those glasses yet, because if I were drinking right now, I'd spew all over the place. From under the rickety wood table, Squid woofs, as if even he's startled.

"Shit, Jerusha, you're..." *Perfect.* "Amazing."

With a smile, she fills the glasses at the sink. "Living room?"

"Sure."

She leads the way and I look my fill, enjoying the sight of her the way I would her smell or taste, or the tight feel of her around me. There's promise in those curves. Heat and power and give.

I want to devour her.

Instead, I sit on the soft, second-hand couch beside her and slug back a full glass of water.

"Dirty talk," she says, as if I need a reminder. I can picture her in class, up front, reminding her teachers of where they left off. I'll bet she's this excited to learn and I'll bet her professors eat it up.

"Just talk."

"Okay." I swear if I gave her a sheet of paper, she'd take notes. "Talk. Yes." She's nodding fast, so studious.

I angle my body toward hers, leaving a frustrating amount of space between us. "First time I saw you, you know what you had on?"

She blinks, as if this isn't what she'd expected. And, frankly, I don't know what the hell I'm doing. I'm not some porno-talking sexpert. I'm just a dude who says shit when he gets riled up. I'm riled up now, so close I can almost smell her. Almost. So close my cock aches, heavy and warm and too constricted in my nice work jeans. So close that if she made a move, I'm not sure I could deny her, despite my best intentions.

"Skirt? T-shirt?"

"One of those long, flowy ones that reaches down to your ankles." I slide an arm over the back of the sofa. "Baggy, paint-stained T-shirt. Hair tied up high on your head with a paintbrush poking out."

"Sometimes a brush is all I've got."

"I know. 'Cause you're so busy."

"Exactly." There's a hint of surprise in that one word, like she didn't think anyone noticed.

"I notice." I let my eyes slide down to her sweet neck, over the ripped collar of her shirt, to where her breasts rise and fall faster than usual. "I notice your nipples are hard right now. Could mean you're cold." My gaze returns to her face. "But I think it means you like this—your body likes this. Me being close, recognizing it. Recognizing you."

Her little tongue slips out to slick over her bottom lip and my mouth drops open. I'm panting and I've done nothing to her. With her. Shit, I've done nothing to myself. But, fuck, I want to reach down and press my palm to my cock.

"First time I saw you, I felt so goddamn guilty."

"Why?"

"Got hard. Watching you work. I had to help you move, just to be... What's the word?"

"Forgiven? Absolved?"

"Yeah. I wanted absolution."

"Granted." Her smirk is filthy.

"Thanks." I let the fingers of my left hand play with a stray curl. It's frizzed out and wild—as off-the-wall different as she is. "You were all sweaty by the end. Both were. It made your shirt stick to your waist, your...breasts."

She bites her lip and shifts, like my words are doing things to her.

"You like me telling you this?"

"Yes. Yes and also..."

I go tight. If she doesn't like it, I'll stop.

"And also, it makes me all...antsy."

"Tell me about that."

"Oh..." Her throat moves like she's thinking about it or going through options. "I get achy when you're around. Like...I need something."

"What?" My body cants forward.

"I get nervous and *very* excited." Another dry-sounding swallow. Her eyes flick over mine, then down and back up, over and over. "Are you hard...now?"

9

JUST LIKE HEAVEN

JERUSHA

He was right, of course. Just talking is getting me riled up. Beyond riled. I may have orgasmed fast earlier, but it's nothing compared to how it would be right now—with his presence and his words.

"So hard it hurts." He's playing with my hair, twisting it and letting it go, petting it with little tugs in between. "Wait. Go back. You said you needed something. What's that?"

He's so close, so big, somehow taller than I realized. And wider. Intimidating...and yet... "I don't know."

I chicken out.

"I feel like I need...your body. Is that weird?"

"No. Not at all. What else?"

"I get wet. Which, I looked up, because I didn't know...I didn't realize it was normal, this feeling? On the internet, I saw that the wetness is on purpose, to make it easier to..." I gulp back the rest, suddenly shy, not at the words so much as the reality it presents. Here, in this moment, I'm wet and he's hard and it could happen. He could slide himself inside me. I could take it. The urge to spread my legs and show him is immense. "I feel empty," I whisper instead.

He growls, drops his head on the back of the sofa, closes his eyes. "I want to slide inside you, Jerusha." I don't expect him to respond like that, but he does, as if he can't talk and watch me at the same time. A thrill runs through me at the idea that I might hold power over this big, strong man.

"I want to run my cock up and down your sweet cunt. Sink in deep." His words steal my breath and my moment of dominance.

A gentle pull at my hair. I drop my head so I'm facing him head-on. All I can do is breathe, hyper-aware of his closeness, his distance, the tightness in my breasts...my lack of underwear. I shift my legs, press them together so he won't smell me.

"Thought you looked young that first day, which made me feel..." He lifts his hand and pats the air. "Wrong. But I guess I've adjusted to that. You're young, but you're...not."

I can't help a little smirk. "I'm glad."

"Fuck. Me, too." Still holding my curl, he strokes the backs of his fingers from my temple down. I twist to meet him with my mouth and let my lips open, let him press one thick knuckle to the inner edge. I don't stop my tongue from touching, tasting, feeling the hard ridges of rough skin and calluses. His gasp urges me on, further down, to the tip of that finger, which I lick and bite.

I'm a shaky, breathless mess of nerves, but his expression gives me courage. He looks utterly lost, like I've stolen his brain and replaced it with pure lust and, since that's exactly what I feel, I go on, kissing, biting, learning, and then it's nothing but his mouth and mine, teeth clashing before some inner rhythm takes over and we're dancing. Together. Heads tilting, tongues twisting, lips ebbing and flowing with our conjoined inner pulse.

I'm panting into his mouth and he's making these low, happy

noises that are closer to animal than human. As close as communication can get.

I *love* it. I knew I would, given the chance, but I love it more than I'd imagined. More than food. Well... I giggle into his mouth and he drinks it up. As much as food. And making art. As much as the smell of fall and floating in water.

What I like about this sensory experience is that it's shared.

And I like who I'm sharing it with.

I'm not sure who pulls away first or if we're so in tune that we do it together. There's enough space for breathing, then smelling, then eye contact, which sizzles so deep in my chest it hurts.

I blink back to the dim room, a light smell of dog, my too-soft sofa.

A car drives by outside, the sound of water under their tires.

I almost can't believe the world's moved on while we kissed. It doesn't seem possible.

"You okay?" Karl watches me, reaches up, pushes a stray curl from my face. Which is good, since I'm not sure I can move my arms yet.

"Amazing."

His smile's sweet and young, making me wish I'd known him as a child. But then the lines around his eyes come into focus, and the sprinkle of grey in his hair, the intensity in his almost-black eyes... No. No, I like this version—weathered and wise and fully aware of who he is. I want to be that self-aware.

"That was..." I let out a long, slow exhale and roll my eyes up to the black ceiling fan that reminds me of him. "Better than I'd imagined."

He chuckles and yawns at the same time.

"Oh, gosh, you must be exhausted. I kept you up so late!"

"*You* kept *me* up late? Next you'll be saying that you corrupted me."

"Obviously I debauched you, Karl. Led you unto evil."

His smile slowly fades, leaving an expression I can't define in its place. "Nothing evil about you, Jerusha. Far from it."

I swallow something back. It's not regret; I'll never feel that around this man. But fear, maybe? Of losing this before it's begun? What is this anyway? A man doing a woman a favor? Whatever. I shove the feelings down, do my best to ignore them, because fear of living's the opposite of what I do now.

Fear is what my parents have, and the rest of my family. Fear of doing something wrong and missing out on the afterlife. Fear of sinning, making mistakes—being human.

I'm not afraid of that. At all. The only thing that scares me is missing opportunities. I promised myself I'd live life to its fullest —here and now, instead of when I die.

I'm truthful in my heart and in my words, and I'm always generous, because what is life for if not sharing? And when have I shared anything so deeply as tonight?

I'm about to lean forward, full of the need to share more with him—my thoughts or another kiss, I don't know—when he lets out a jaw-cracking yawn.

"Definitely past my bedtime." He stands and stretches, with a third yawn.

I let him pull me to my feet and flat against his chest, wondering if being close to him will always make my pulse race.

I hope so.

"You're magic, Jerusha Graff."

"That mean you'll do it again? Lessons, I mean?"

Grimacing, he opens his mouth as if to say something and stops. "Let's play it by ear." He gives a tight smile. "Tomorrow, you'll probably meet some young guy who pushes all the right buttons. Won't need me," he says, with grim certainty.

"Oh. Sure."

I accompany him to the back door, painfully aware of my near-nudity and the wetness coating my thighs. Squid races out, but Karl stalls. He bends toward me, setting my heart to flapping in my chest like a bird. When he kisses my cheek instead of my lips, the feeling turns sour.

"Sleep tight, Jerusha."

"Okay, Karl. You, too."

He throws me a smile and takes off, leaving me wondering what I did wrong.

I stew on that for a while and then pick up my phone.

10

COME AS YOU ARE

KARL

I close her back gate and run my hands over my face, breathing too hard for the short distance I just walked. This isn't the way this is supposed to go.

Dammit. I don't do this shit. I don't lose control over a kiss. A smile.

This was about *her*, not me.

Then why the fuck am I sporting a rock-hard boner outside a girl's house at whatever o'clock in the morning instead of getting much-needed sleep?

'Cause I'm a moron.

And this has got to stop.

Whistling for Squid, I head to my place, unlock the gate, and go inside, all business.

I manage to keep up the charade through my shower, but my phone buzzes as I slide naked into bed, still hard as nails, and I snatch it up, finally admitting that I've got to face the truth: this isn't just a fucked-up favor to help a cute neighbor out.

I want her.

I open my messaging app, unreasonably excited to see Jerusha's name pop up.

I hope this doesn't wake you up, but I was wondering a couple things...

Oh, shit. I wait for what's next, caught in a mixed-up limbo of my own creation.

1. Did I do something wrong earlier? Or is that just...how people leave things? And 2. Is there more to dirty talk? I think we got sidetracked and I'd like to learn. If you're still okay with it, of course. :-)

"Fuck!" I mutter, staring at the screen.

Squid woofs from his dog bed.

"It's okay boy, I just... The hell am I supposed to do?"

He responds with a low whine, clearly wondering what's gotten into me in the middle of the night.

I drop the phone on the bed, shut my eyes and press my fingers hard to my eyeballs, begging my brain to come up with a solution.

I've just picked the phone up to call the whole thing off when it vibrates in my hand.

My dick reacts before I've read the damn thing, pulsing like she's in the room with me.

I'm still wet, thinking about you.

Goddamn. I swallow and reach down to give myself a squeeze. As if she needs lessons.

Two choices hang in the dark in front of me: The obvious one, which is to shut this thing down, now, before someone gets hurt. And the other one; the one my cock's rooting for. Dive in dick-first.

I put my finger to the screen and type.

Can I call?

Yes.

I hit her name.

"Hi."

"Hey."

"Sorry, I—"

"Jerusha, I—"

"Yes?"

"You did nothing wrong. I left because I feel like..." I sigh, looking for the right word. "You know the joke from earlier? You debauching me? Well, I'm pretty sure I'm the one corrupting you."

"Corrupting? No." She lets out a laugh that I've never heard from her before, like a low, sexy sample of what's got to be her bedroom voice. "Do you have any idea what I had to do when I got home from your restaurant earlier?"

As if I weren't listening closely enough already, my ears prick up even further. "Tell me."

"I had to..." She swallows, and that second or two of delay makes me absolutely wild. "Touch myself. Because of you." There's accusation in her tone. It lights me up in ways I couldn't begin to understand.

"Shit."

She snuffles.

"Go ahead. Tell me about what you did."

"Oh, I... Can you... Would you say *the thing* first?"

"The thing?"

"The corrupting thing. The one that will ruin me. I want to be debauched, Karl. I want you to do it."

I let out a choked laugh. Who's corrupting who here?

But fuck it. She wants it. Who am I to baby her? She's already got over-protective parents. I'm just the guy next door.

Then again, I'm feeling mighty over-protective toward her, or at least possessive. "I'm bossy, Jerusha. Okay? Should never have brought this up, 'cause I'm bossy and pushy and...hell, I'm also a bit of an asshole."

"No you're not."

"Especially in bed. And probably on the phone, if I let it happen that way."

"I don't..." She stops for a second or two, like she's trying to figure out what I'm saying. "I don't know what that means. Or looks like or—"

"It means, if I do this the way I'd do it with..." Another woman? Hell, no. This one. "If I do this my way, it won't be pretty."

"That's the version I want."

Fine. "Good, then stop talking right now," I say, voice low and gruff and mean as hell. My cock's on board with the shift in tone. "And listen to me."

"Yes," she says; a whisper that I wish I could see on her lips, read in her eyes.

"Good." I wrap my hand around my dick and stroke it, hard.

"Wait."

I take my hand off.

"You like to be in charge, but I led, that first time. The kiss on my porch."

"Yeah." I snort. "Don't get used to it." My hand's already back to its stroking. "I'm touching myself. Thinking of you. You got your hand between your legs?"

"No."

"Do it."

Her breathing changes, goes choppy and weird as a long, raspy, moan comes through the phone.

"Wait. Hold on. What are you wearing?"

"My nightshirt."

I picture that worn out little thing and jerk myself again. "Panties?"

"No."

"Good. Touch yourself." After a few seconds, I go on. "Just remember, what I like isn't what everyone wants, okay? It's me. Not you. If you're not comfortable, let me know."

Maybe I'll go too far and she'll end this thing. I'm almost relieved at the idea.

"What about *you*, Karl? What do you have on?" *Of course* she turns the tables on me.

Shaking my head, I reply. "Nothing. Just my hand on my erection, you in my brain."

She releases a harsh exhale. Almost a laugh. "Feels like I'm diving into the deep end with you."

"You are. Hell, I like a little confrontation with my sex. Some push and pull." I'm stroking myself fast and hard, wondering how dark I'll get before she folds. "I want to decide what happens. Got that?"

"Oh..." She exhales in fits and starts, like maybe her body's moving to a quick rhythm, too.

I shut my eyes, picturing her hand under a blanket her tits jostling with each move.

What I can't figure out is why she won't shut this down. I lower my voice. "Got it, Jerusha?"

She whimpers. "Yes. You're the boss. Yes."

"Good." I almost groan at the sounds she makes. "Now say my name."

"Karl."

"Good. Again."

"Karl," she moans long and low and lost, just the way I've imagined.

Like a switch flipping, I'm no longer trying to push her away. Hell, I want this. More than that. I *need* it.

"Yeah." I give myself a few good pulls, enough to squeeze a drop of precum from the tip. It makes my hand glide easier. "Dammit. I want to say dirty shit to you."

"Yes. Yes, do it. Say filthy things."

"You asked for it." It's a warning, an accusation. "I keep thinking about that pussy of yours, Jerusha. About how tight it'll be. How swollen and pink."

I listen through a series of high whimpers and go on, already half-addicted to the sound of her. "Fuck, I wanna taste it; all that wetness you've got for me." Now it's my turn to groan. "I *smelled* you, tonight, you know? Did you do that on purpose, huh? Come to the door with no panties on?"

"No. No, I—"

"You sure? 'Cause I liked that little nightie. I liked the way it hid you, but gave me access."

"I didn't mean—"

"Oh you meant it. Waiting up for me like a—" I clamp up, shut my mouth and eyes, and hold my breath for a count of ten. No way am I calling her names, no matter what I warned. No matter what my inner asshole's begging for.

"Like what?" she asks, sounding eager and breathless.

"Like a..." I scour my brain for something that won't make this feel wrong. "A dirty girl, waiting for me wet and ready."

"I am. I mean, I want to be. Your dirty girl. *Yours*, Karl." I drop my phone and fumble it back up to my ear.

"Shit, Jerusha, you're..." *Good at this*, I almost say, but that would pull her out of the moment, make her self-conscious, which is the last thing I want. I catch my breath, do my best to control the need racing from my brain to my cock and back. "Dirty. Just for me. Nobody else gets this." I'm losing it, going way too far, too fast. Almost believing half the shit I say. Almost believing she's mine.

Her *Yes* eggs me on and, though I know better, I let it all out. "That little snatch in the open, soaking wet, smelling like sex after you touched yourself. D'you come thinking about me? Huh? D'you rub yourself raw? Cream on your hand, imagining me as your—" *Daddy*.

I pull back, grunting with effort. *What the fuck?* This isn't somewhere my brain's gone before and though, hell, I'd be into it, I can't imagine she would.

Time to put a stop to this. I swallow back the filth trying to make its way from my mouth.

"My what?" she whispers, all high and breathy. "What were you going to say?"

I clear my throat. "What do you think?"

"I think..." She swallows, like she's parched. Or hungry. Or gagging for what I have to give her. "I don't know."

"Right. That's...that's fine." I give my shaft a tight, quelling squeeze. "Okay. Let's, uh... You doing okay? How do you feel?"

"I feel empty."

My erection pulses. My mouth takes off without me. "Yeah. You need me."

"Yes."

"Say it," I bite out through clamped teeth.

"I need you...inside me." She gasps. "Karl."

"Yeah." The image blasts through me—her open and waiting on all fours, pink cunt glistening for me. Just me. I'd grip her hips, steadying her. Push in. That first press of my cockhead, almost painful in its intensity. "You've never taken a cock. Never felt what it's like."

"No. No... Will it hurt?"

"I'll make it good."

"How?"

I almost lose myself in the endless possibilities. Her sweet, plush body's the sexiest thing I've ever seen. "I'll eat your pussy. Lick it, suck you till you scream."

She says something incomprehensible. About to lose it, I'd bet.

"Put me on speaker."

"Mm?"

"Speaker. I want to hear everything."

"Everything?"

"Your hands, your pussy. How soaking wet you are."

"Oh... O-okay."

I do the same and put the phone down, almost laughing at the cramp in my hand.

I spit in my palm and, because I want her to know just how lewd I can get, I tell her. "I'm using saliva...as lube." I run one slick fist from my crown to the bottom of my cock, grabbing my balls with the other. Every move is exaggerated, every noise magnified for her listening pleasure. "Do it."

"What?"

"Spit. In your hand."

When she does, the sound has me picturing things—her face over my dick, my hand in her hair. Her little tongue, all over me, lapping me up. Sucking me deep. Would she do that?

Talk about corruption. Would I let her? What is it about this woman that makes me want to take things too far?

"Use it to touch yourself. Make it so easy."

A groan slices from my phone, straight through the air and into my lungs. I have the irrational desire to jump out of bed and race over there.

That urge ramps things up, pushes me further. "I've been rock-hard for hours, Jerusha. Since you pranced into my restaurant, all smiley and fresh." On a date with another man. I growl. "Now I'm picturing you with that pussy out, just waiting for me. Did you wait up for me tonight 'cause you wanted me to fuck you? Hm? D'you text me so I'd come over and make you come again?"

"Y-yes." Filthy, wet sounds. "Yes, Karl."

"Fuck," I whisper, working myself fast and hard. "Dirty girl."

"I...I am."

"What?" I slow, barely able to focus through the haze of want, the need to come.

"I'm a dirty girl. A...oh, God, I'm a s-slut. Your dirty little slut."

Holy *hell*, where did that come from?

"Good," I grit out. "Now stuff a finger into your tight hole."

"Into my...my..."

"Do it. Put a finger in your cunt, Jerusha. I want to hear you."

"Oh... Oh, God."

I stop jerking and listen. The sounds are unbearably explicit. A whole new dimension to sex that I'd never fully appreciated. "Good. Another."

"It's... I'm..."

"Do it. Two fingers. Stretch that pussy for me. Get it ready."

More wet sounds, more high, frantic whimpering.

"Close your eyes."

"O-okay."

"Push in, nice and slow, the way you'll take my cock." I palm myself again, start a stroke, up and back. If I time it just right, with the current soundtrack, I'm almost there, in her room, against her body—not quite inside her, but easing myself between her pussy lips.

"Yes, yes."

"Say my name."

"Karl."

"Yeah." I grip myself until my fist could almost be her. "I'm fucking you so hard."

"It's tight, Karl."

"Not tight enough. Three fingers."

"I... I can't..."

"Don't make me come over there." The threat pings all around me, my muscles ready to spring into action, to race to her, buck naked, and *make* her take three fingers. Maybe more. "My hands are bigger than yours. Won't be easy if I have to do it in person."

"Oh...oh..." The rhythm of her hand's taken over now, I can hear the slick slide, the sharp inhalations. I want to smell her, frustrated that I can't. I shut my eyes and imagine how good this would be, up close. "It's...it's in, Karl."

"Good. Tell me how I feel."

"Too much." She shudders. "Good. So good."

"Yeah. We'll make it work." My balls are high and tight. I pull them, just enough to drag this out.

"Oh, God. It's coming. I'm almost there."

"Good." I let go of my balls and start jerking hard, the final stretch right in front of me. "Say my name."

"Karl. It's close." She sounds frantic, close to scared.

"Fuck. I'm close, too." I tighten my fist, to the point of pain, like I've got to suffer for what I'm doing here. It's that fucking wrong. "I'm coming for you. Will you? Will you do it for me?" There's something almost plaintive in the way I ask. Like I'm begging. I am. I'm fucking begging for it and then, because, hell, she should know what effect she has, I say it. "Fuck, Jerusha. Do it. Come for me. Please."

I screw my eyes shut and let go.

Abruptly, everything goes quiet.

Jerusha

My mouth's open, but I can't breathe. My eyes are wide, I can't see. Every muscle in my body's seized up and there's nothing I can do but take it. The way he made me take my own fingers.

Pleasure like I've never experienced before. Forced on me, from me, squeezed from my body. I'm not just fluttering, the way I have in the past. This time, the orgasm's gripped me around the neck and I swear I lose a handful of seconds before floating back to earth.

Maybe longer, judging from the silence on the other end. Did I miss our goodbyes? Has he hung up and called it a night?

"Karl?" I reach for the phone. It's almost pitch-black in my room, broken only by a swathe of light from the street lamp outside. I'm still shaking, slick with sweat though it's not entirely warm in here. "You still there?" I can hardly get the words out through my own panting.

His reply's a low chuckle that sends a shiver through my limp limbs. "Yeah."

"That was...amazing."

"Good." Just that word gives me another aftershock. Like he's conditioned me to respond to *good* and *yeah*...and his name.

"Karl," I say, just to see what happens.

He growls, I shiver. We're a regular orchestra.

"You okay? After doing that?"

"I'm amazing." And because—why not be honest?—I tell him. "If orgasms had a hierarchy, that one would be Gold. No, wait. Is platinum the best?"

"Gold's good," he rumbles. "Save platinum for the real event."

As if caught by surprise, my insides tighten up around nothing. The real event.

"Are we...will you..." I shut my eyes. "Will you show me that, too?"

His lack of answer punches me like a ball to the belly. Sudden tears prickle my sinuses. Which is silly, given what we've done. I gather myself, doing my best to ignore the hurt. "Well, thank you. For the...wait. Was that phone sex?"

"Yeah. Yeah, it was."

"So, a two for one. Dirty talk *and* phone sex."

"There you go." His voice is harder, almost businesslike. More awake or unhappy?

"Well, thank you."

He clears his throat. "Any time."

Does he mean that? Because I'd honestly keep going, despite the late hour. I glance at the phone. Oh crap. I have to be up in like three hours.

"All right," I say, unsuccessfully stifling a yawn. "Good night.

"Night, Jerusha."

I'm about to end the call when his voice comes through. "Oh, and Jerusha."

"Yeah?"

"You're not a, uh..." He clears his throat. "You're not a slut. You know that, right?"

"I know." I giggle. "I don't believe in that anyway."

"Sluts?"

"Shaming people."

"Good," he says, low and rough enough to light another fire inside.

I open my mouth to ask if there'll be another session, but he's already talking.

"Sleep tight, Jerusha."

I open my mouth to respond and he's gone.

11

DON'T SPEAK

JERUSHA

As if I weren't exhausted enough, everything goes haywire the next morning. I don't have time to pack my lunch and spend my entire morning fighting the growling in my belly. I dye a batch of wool, which, due to inattention, ends up poop brown instead of purple. And I almost get run over, crossing on a red light, on the way to meet my friends in our favorite coffee shop. The driver screams insults at me for a good twenty seconds before taking off too fast down Grace Street.

Which should burst my bubble, given how lewd it was. Ironically, it feeds the hunger. And not for food this time. It's my hunger for Karl that's doing my head in. I've thought about him constantly, in a half-dream state, where my body's this lush, heavy thing, filled with want, and bad words are things that he might say to turn me on.

Would he call me the things that driver called me? Would I like it coming from Karl's mouth?

You do that on purpose, huh? Come to the door with no panties on?

I keep thinking about the things he said. Keep shivering like he's beside me. Touching me.

Dirty girl, waiting for me...half-naked.

Would I like it from Karl's mouth?

The answer's in the way my body responds at just the notion. It's all jittery and excited. I want dirty, I want crass. And yeah, I'd like all the bad words from Karl.

I'm the one who said the S word, after all. I burn up, just thinking about that. Probably blushing to high heaven.

I'm a dirty girl. Your dirty little slut.

Another wave of heat floods me, part embarrassment, part excitement. Strangely, the embarrassed thing almost makes the excitement...more. The two sensations, intertwined, are incendiary.

But then that other thing creeps in—worry or fear or whatever it is that swamped me after last night's goodbye.

Another brand of embarrassment, only this one is painful rather than titillating. A little pathetic, if I'm being honest. Because this whole thing's not dating or flirting or going out. It's not two people working on a relationship, sexual or otherwise.

It's my neighbor letting me use him to explore sex. And, sure, he's gotten into it a time or two, but does he really want me?

Karl

Everything reminds me of Jerusha today. The bright oranges and reds and yellows of the leaves, someone whizzing by on a bicycle, the half-hard state of my own dick. In the coffee shop, I wait in line, wondering if she likes coffee, or if she's more of a tea person. And then I try to guess what kind of tea she'd drink and if she'd like the hot toddies I've been working on at the bar, which reminds me of—

"Dad."

"Hm?" I blink back to the present.

"Are you kidding me right now?" Harper joins me in the coffee shop line and snaps her blue-tipped fingers right in my face.

"Oh, hey! Harper!"

"Don't *Oh, hey, Harper* me! I've been yelling for the last like *seventeen* minutes." Which translates to maybe thirty seconds. She turns to take in the people sitting around inside, barely glancing my way as she goes on. "What's wrong with you?"

"Nothing. I'm good."

Another look around and she sees someone she knows. "Oh. Hey! It's Mikey! Grab me a pumpkin thingy, will you?"

"Wait, a muffin or a..."

She rolls her eyes. "A latte. Pumpkin spice."

"With whip?"

A snort this time—I'm getting full-on teenage Harper and I kinda like it. I've missed my baby these past few months. "Does the pope shit in the woods?"

Now it's my turn to roll my eyes and shake my head. You'd think she was brought up by barbarians. I glance down at my ripped work clothes and filthy shitkickers, my hands sporting the homemade tats I gave myself as a kid. Maybe she was.

I step up and order my coffee and her mocha whatever with a couple muffins, turn and take in the room, which I can honestly say I hadn't noticed in the slightest.

Even now, I barely register the faces I scan, until I reach Harper.

She's talking to a couple people I don't know. A few years older than her, maybe. One is slender, with long, dark hair and a long face. Pretty. The other is shorter and plumper and blonde with pink and red and purple streaks. They look like art students.

"Karl!" My name's called. I grab the stuff and head over to my daughter, just as the door opens, letting a whirlwind inside. I swear the barometric pressure changes. All eyes swing to the front.

Jerusha.

A can't help the grin that splits my face in half. She turns, looking for someone—not me, since we hadn't planned to meet here, but a part of me wants her to light up the way I have. And she does. Just not at me.

She's looking at Harper. No, the people with Harper.

"Hey, you guys!" she squeals from the across the room, then barrels towards us. Maybe five feet from where I'm standing, she sees me and comes to a dead stop.

If this were a movie, someone would drop a tray of glasses. The music would scratch to silence. All eyes would be on us.

She's not smiling at me. Not the way she did for them. She's watching me, wary.

"Morning, Jerusha."

"Hi." The smile she gives me is completely different. A little hesitant, a little shy. But it's all for me, and I like it. "Karl."

My heart picks up speed at the sound of my name in her voice. I take an unconscious step toward her, she draws closer. The hum around us becomes nothing but a backdrop.

"You sleep okay?" It's all I can think of to say. Here I am, the father of a practically full-grown human, and all I can do is grin and ask dumb questions.

"Yes." She nods, mouth compressed, cheeks bright pink.

Her eyes slide down to the coffees and pastries in my arms and back up. I should put this stuff down so I can touch her.

No. No, I shouldn't. My daughter's here.

"You, uh, meeting someone? Or you want to..." I turn to the table where Harper and her friends have sat down.

"Well, that's my date. Mikey."

Date. I blink, feeling slow. "Mikey?"

"The person next to Harper. The other is Alba."

Understanding dawns. "Oh. Okay." Should I be jealous? Because I am.

From the table, their low voices carry.

"My dad," I hear Harper say in her not-so-quiet secretive voice.

"*Well*, now. He is a stone cold—"

"Don't say it."

"He knows Jerusha?"

"*You* know Jerusha, Mikey?" Harper asks.

"The three of us do grad work together," says the person named Mikey. Jerusha's date.

"You gonna hand me that coffee, Dad, or do I need to stand up and get it?"

It's my turn to blush, which is ridiculous. The whole thing's ridiculous. I look at the little round table—my daughter, her friends, Jerusha hovering, the four of them half my age. I can't do this. "Gotta go." I nod, hand the shit over to Harper, mumble some kind of goodbye to Jerusha, and make a beeline for the door.

"Wait! Dad! Stop!"

Out on the sidewalk, I pause, breathing hard. A scalding sip of coffee does nothing to improve my mood.

"What the hell, Dad?"

"It's... This place is too damn small."

"This place?"

"Richmond." My mouth closes, out of self-preservation more than anything else. I can't tell my daughter what I'm doing. They're the same generation. The same fucking friend group. "It's fine. I'm fine."

"Dad." Harper slaps my shoulder and holds it. "Seriously. If you're gonna date her, you're gonna have to get used to this."

"We're not dating," is all I manage. It sounds immature and feels wrong. "We're..."

"Way-way-way-way-wait. I can't express the extent to which

I need *no* information about what's going on with you and my new mom."

I get a snort out before she goes on, closer now, but still semi-shouting, like she's trying to get her words through my thick, dumb skull. "I've never seen you into a woman, Dad. Like never ever ever, not in a million years ev—."

"Good. No reason you should know anything about *that*."

"But you *like* her. Don't tell me you're just hanging out, okay? Oh, no strings. Casual. Whatever. Don't you dare be all cold, distant asshole, 'cause I'll tell you that is not what you brought me up to—"

"Harper." She stops. Thank God. "*She's* the one who..." *Asked me to teach her sex* isn't something I can exactly say to my daughter. I go with, "Requested a casual thing."

She blinks and turns to look back through the big glass window, obviously offended. "*Seriously?*" My feisty daughter. Mad at me one second, mad for me the next. We were a mess when she was little, her mom and I, falling apart at the seams, but we must have done something right, because I admire this little woman, so damn much.

I shake my head with a smile and lean in. "You don't have to tell me she's special. Okay, kiddo? I know that."

Her eyes go big. "So, you like her."

I smile and squint, trying to see inside. There's nothing but shadows, except for a splash of red and yellow that has got to be today's sweater. "I do. I like her."

Harper inhales, clearly satisfied. She hands me my muffin—which I don't remember giving her—and nudges my arm. "Go do your thing at the bank."

"You don't want to—"

"I want to go in there and get the other side of the story."

"You said you didn't—"

"Go!" She nudges me away.

I should be worried about what's going to be shared, but what I am is jealous.

Some weird proprietary urge makes me take out my phone and send Jerusha a text.

Sorry I ran out.

I understand. It was a lot.

Those dots appear, telling me she's got more to say. I wait, anxious.

When's lesson 2?

Relief floods me.

It occurs to me that I should probably be teaching her how to play hard to get. Give her insight into all the rules and the games people play to torture each other. The hellish misery of going out with people in the modern world.

Ignoring all that, I respond with what I actually want.

Tonight?

I'd like that. What's Lesson 2?

My mind races.

Heavy petting. But isn't this lesson 3?

Let's see. Kissing, dirty talk, heavy petting. You're right! My place at 6?

Sure.

I can't wait.

I slide my phone into my pocket, trying to concentrate on my upcoming meeting with the bank.

After less than a minute, I pull it out again.

Me neither, I type out, grinning wide.

12

SCENARIO

JERUSHA

Heavy petting. What is that? What have I just agreed to? I look up, smile still plastered on my face, wondering if I've got time to look it up before going back to the table.

It takes a sec for me to realize that Mikey, Alba, and Harper are all staring from our corner table. "What?"

"Is my dad texting you?"

I open my mouth and shut it. Mikey rolls their eyes and smacks Harper on the hand. "Don't make me regret letting you sit at our table."

"It's fine," I say, though I'd really been looking forward to some time alone with my friends. There's a lot to talk about.

I settle in my seat, facing the room. We love this table with its semi-private feel, even when the place is packed. My friends and I have spilled a lot of secrets in this spot. At least they have. I mostly listen. I have a feeling that's about to change.

"Sure?" Harper asks. "I can go."

"No. No, it's truly fine."

"Good." She smiles. "Because my dad really likes you."

My face goes up in flames and, rather than stammer out something silly, I take a too-big sip of scalding tea.

Once I'm done coughing, they lean in. "Is this Hot Neighbor?" Mikey asks. "Did you finally ask him out?"

I glance at Harper. "I mean, not in so many words, but..."

"Hot neighbor is a big ole *Daddy*," sings Alba.

My insides go *wild* at that word.

"Hey! That's my father you're—"

Mikey exchanges a look with Alba and then turns to Harper with their signature *get with it* expression. Harper shuts her mouth. "Your father is hot fucking stuff, Harper." Mikey smiles and the expression's pure delight. "Shoulda known, though. You're tall and gorgeous. Got hot genes."

Harper rolls her eyes and looks away.

"You are hot. You know that, right?" Mikey laughs. "Hell, I'd date you if you were my age."

Harper's quick to recover. "Oh, *ahem*." Her eyes flick to me and back to Mikey. "However old you are, Mikey, I'm guessing we're closer in age than this one and my cradle-robbing father." She points a thumb at me.

"Cradle-robbing? This was my idea!" My protests go unheard.

Mikey leans close to Harper, full of sharp intent. "How old *are* you?"

Wait. Am I watching a flirtation here? My attention goes back and forth between them, fascinated. When I finally cross gazes with Alba, her expression mirrors my curiosity.

"Eighteen," says Harper. "You?"

"Twenty-four."

"See? Six years." Harper turns to me. "How much of a gap between you and my dad?"

"Oh. Uh...seventeen."

"So fucking sexy," Alba says.

Harper grimaces.

I stand. "I'd better go."

"No way," Mikey says.

"We want details."

My eyes fly to Harper. "I don't think this is—"

It's Harper's turn to stand. "I get it. *Fine.*"

"Wait up, Harper. I'll walk you out." Mikey throws me a smirk and follows Harper out onto the sidewalk while I sit down, shaking my head.

"Is Mikey picking her up?"

"Yep," replies Alba, shaking her head with a grin. She's got these big, innocent-looking brown eyes—the perfect foil for her deeply kinky soul. I've learned more about sex in the months since I met these two than I'd heard in my entire life. Or imagined.

My brows wrinkle as Mikey returns to their seat, smirk still in place.

"You're not messing around with her, are you?" Alba asks.

"Who, moi?" Mikey's eyes land on me.

"Seriously, Mikey, that's the daughter of my..."

They lean forward. "Yes? Please finish that sentence."

I let my face fall into my palms. "I don't know what he is, you guys."

"He's a fucking daddy, I told you. Big Daddy Karl."

"Mikey's right. Stone cold daddy."

My innards squish again at that word. I dare to look at them through my fingers. "What's that mean, exactly? Can you two explain? 'Cause he's not my father."

"Hell, no, but he could be your daddy. Is he? Is that what this is?"

My mouth drops open. Nothing comes out, which I can tell they both love. Talking sex is kind of their thing. And talking sex with me—whom they call an innocent slut—is their absolute favorite. Shocking and titillating in equal measures.

It's probably as far from my old life as I can get and it's

wonderful—free, open communication about something that's always been painfully taboo.

Slut. I get red, just remembering how I used that word last night.

"Look. Can you explain, please? The daddy references?" *And tell me why I like it so much?*

"It's a real thing. More or less kinky, depending."

"On what?"

"Okay." Alba takes over. "So, you know how we've talked about Dominance?"

"Right, you think I'm a secret submissive."

"Not that secret."

"Do you agree?" I turn to Mikey, who just shrugs.

I deadpan. "Go on."

"We haven't discussed role play, but..." Alba widens her eyes at me, batting those lashes. "Family play is a thing."

Family play. I mouth the words, then stop, mouth open.

"Methinks she likes it." Mikey's voice is low, secretive.

"See?" Alba meets their eyes before looking at me again "So that's one version of it. But that's not what I mean about this guy —unless, hey, maybe it's your thing?"

"I don't know."

"You'll figure it out," Alba says with a matter-of-fact confidence that I adore. "What we're talking about is when an older man, you know, maybe tells you what to do? Maybe takes care of you? There's a lot of potential there. So many ways a daddy kink can pan out. A lot can happen."

"Oh!" Mikey's fingers dance at all the possibilities. "Sugar daddies, for example. They take care of their partner, give them money, gifts, in exchange for sex."

"Oh, no." I shake my head. "No, no, no. Not my thing."

Alba's high-pitched giggle draws people's attention. "Not a sugar daddy, then."

Mikey tilts their head, eyes narrowed. "That's not his vibe, anyway."

"What kind of da—" I lower my voice, casting a glance around us. "*Daddy* does he seem like?"

Mikey gets that bright, avid look in their dark eyes. They lean way in, put their forehead on my shoulder, and whisper, "He looks like a *take-no-shit-boss* of a daddy, who'll tell you what to do and make you like it." Pulling back to give me a long, squinty stare, they go on. "Am I right?"

Alba nods, knowingly.

My mouth drops open. "How did you know?"

"Is that a yes?" Mikey asks.

"Maybe." I draw out the word, holding my smile inside. It's embarrassed, excited, and a little secret.

"Oh, thank you God." Alba's eyes flick heavenward, then back to me. "This is gonna be so good. You don't do shit halfway, do you, Jerusha? Straight into the deep end."

"We need details. You asked him out and now you're, what?" Mikey squints. "A thing? Dating? Fuck buddies? I mean, you've got chemistry out the butthole. Saw it from a mile off. He didn't kiss you, though, so—"

"I asked him to teach me."

Alba's eyes get huge. "Teach you."

"How to kiss and do other...sex things."

"He's teaching you how to sex?" At my nod, Mikey's jaw drops. They go completely still, throw a look at Alba, and let out a slow, audible breath. "Fuck. Me. Holy shit, honey. This is the hottest thing."

"Seriously." I've never seen Alba this excited. "Do you have any idea? You probably blundered right into his big daddy kink. Look at you, all innocent with those baby blues and freckles and he gets to show you the ropes."

"She's blushing." Mikey's eyes go sharp. "Hold on, wait.

Don't tell me you did it. Have you *done* it? Without letting us know?"

I shake my head.

"Oh, thank God," Mikey mutters.

"So, what's happened?"

"We, um, kissed."

"Nice. Good." Mikey's smile is happy. "You liked it, obviously."

"Yes. Wow. *Yes*."

"Okay and..."

"We dirty talked. On the phone. Like, sexting, I mean phone sex."

"Did you come?" Alba watches me, avidly.

I nod, glad the nearest table's too far to hear. Hopefully. I mean, I love these conversations, but usually they're focused on my friends' sex lives, not mine.

I've never had a sex life before. That I might have one now makes me giddy.

"What about him? Did he come?"

"Yes. I think so. He called me a...dirty girl and then I told him I was his..." My voice descends to the barest of whispers. "*Slut*."

Alba gives Mikey a look that screams *told you so* without words.

"Wow. Okay. And he knows you've never..." I nod and watch the corners of Mikey's lips tighten, like there's a smile just dying to come out. "And..." Brows up, Mikey's expressive hands circle between us, trying to draw me out.

"And I liked it. I liked it, okay, guys? It was unbelievable."

"Good."

I shiver at that word, memories of Karl saying it last night, full of heat and approval. I'm already programmed as surely as one of Pavlov's dogs to react.

"What is it?" Alba leans closer. "What's wrong, then?"

"He's... I think he's just being nice to me."

Mikey's laugh bursts out low and knowing. "Yeah, no."

"No?"

"No, honey. No. The chemistry..." They pat their cheeks. "Do you see my skin? I'm burning up. Blushing. Still. From the flames you two set off. Okay? No. This isn't one-sided. You can call it teaching or messing around or pretending that he's *Doing you a favor*," they add air quotes. "But lady, nothing about that man is just nice. Nothing."

"And that's good?"

"Chemistry with an older, more mature guy who knows what he's doing in the bed and can talk filth? That's the trifecta," Alba says. "It's what you want."

Mikey leans back. "God, if I could have had that the first time, instead of..."

"Instead of what?"

"Messy fumbling with Sissy Carter in the back of my mom's minivan. Or the time I gave Evan Schmidt oral in the mall Friday's bathroom."

"Wow." I can't help the fresh wave of heat that takes over at Mikey's descriptions. Always titillating and unexpected and unfailingly unapologetic. Alba's even more detailed—and daring—when she talks about her experiences.

That's my favorite thing about our conversations—sex without guilt. The opposite of everything I grew up with. Our discussions feel clean, somehow. Sweet and natural. Like this is the way things are meant to be, out in the open, instead of buried under sin and embarrassment and shame.

"I love your stories. Both of you."

"You're a perfect audience," Alba says. "Curious, open. Ready to try things."

"Daddy Karl must be in heaven."

"Yeah, so what's next?"

I take a shaky breath. "We've got plans for tonight."

"Plans? Like doing the deed?"

"Tonight is lesson number three. Heavy petting. *His* words. I have no idea what it means. I can look it up if—"

"It's foreplay, honey," Mikey says happily. "And what it means, if you're lucky, is that Big Daddy's going down."

Alba cackles, slapping both hands on the table so hard the coffee sloshes. "Oh, *please* let's call him Cunnilingus Karl."

"Here's to heavy petting," Mikey gives me a Cheshire cat grin, "with Cunnilingus Karl."

13

HEY DADDY

KARL

She opens the door and, though I didn't expect a repeat of last night's outfit, I'm half disappointed that she's fully clothed.

"Hi, Karl." Her smile, the way she lowers her head a little, and bites that plump lip, eyes still on mine—that's all pure, perfect Jerusha. It hits me in the gut. I'm almost sick with anticipation.

If I didn't know myself, I'd say there's a good dose of nerves mixed up with the excitement. And, hell, maybe so. There's pressure in what I'm here to do. Got to get it right, don't I?

"Hey." I lift the pizza and beer and wine I picked up earlier. "Dinner."

Her pixie smile loosens some of my tension. I'm not here to teach her rocket science. We're gonna make out. That's it.

"Heavy Petting 101," I say, flippant as fuck.

"Oh." Her blush deepens. "Right. Should we...are you sure you want to eat? I mean, do you have time, or maybe you just want to—"

"Let's eat." I give a nonchalant shrug and meet her eyes. "Make it like a real date. Good practice for you."

"Of course. Like a real date."

"Second date." My lips go into a deep, automatic frown. "Make that fourth. You might not want to do it too soon. If you..." *Shut up, dumbass.*

I shut the door as she grabs the pizza and heads back to the kitchen, reminding me of a similar scene, just the other night. With notable differences. Like, oh, say, the things we've said to each other in the past twenty-four hours. And, hell, the fact that we've heard each other come. I know, for example, that she stops breathing at the specific moment it happens. Stops moving at all.

I want to see that intensity, maybe put my hand to her throat and feel her go still, press my mouth to hers; get a deep taste of her pleasure.

"...without Squid?"

"Sorry." I shake myself. "What was that?"

"You didn't bring Squid along?"

"Oh, nah. Figured it'd be better if..." I trail off. Maybe she doesn't need to know all of my thought processes.

"Better if he's not here?"

"He, uh, gets curious. Sticks his nose where it doesn't belong."

"Wow! Okay, yes. I hadn't thought of that."

I force a laugh. "No manners."

We set the pizza up on plates, each grab a drink and head to the living room, without a word. Impossible to tell if it's awkward between us or comfortable. I hope the latter, but, aside from work and family and the very occasional screw, I spend no time with women.

I sit on the sofa, she sinks to the floor and it's confirmed—shit's weird.

"Uh, Jerusha, do you—"

"Don't feel like you have to—"

"Sorry?"

"Say that again?"

We laugh, definitely awkward, and come to a stop.

In the silence that follows, I set my plate down and bend forward. "You okay? After last night?"

She nods, watching me. "I'm good. Are you?"

Just as I'm about to give her an automatic yes, I stop and reconsider. How do I feel about this situation? Do I like it?

Hell, no. Like is too small a word for what's happening in my body right now. Not that I'm particularly good at expressing feelings, but she's this ball of honesty. It's the least I can do to try.

"I'm...uh... I'm kinda tired. But in a good way, you know?"

Her smile's somehow knowing and cheerful and dirty all at once. "Same. And I can't stop thinking about..."

"Come here." I half dive to the floor and she arches up and my hands dig into all that hair and hers are on my neck and shoulder and our mouths meet and, Jesus, I'm not hungry for pizza or any of this other shit, but for her.

The kiss isn't choreographed, but it's just right. The taste and smell and sounds of her are a cocktail made for me.

And the feel, shit, how could I forget the way she presses and pulls back, nips and licks, like she needs to try all the things, do it all, taste it all. Like she's got only so long to live and—

I pull back, out of breath. "You're not, I don't know, dying or something are you?"

Her comically startled expression tells me what a jackass I am.

"Uh, no?" Those massive eyes get even wider. "Are you?"

"No. Shit, no." I rub my hands over my face and sink back into the sofa. "Though my brain's gone haywire."

When she doesn't reply, I suck in a big breath and look at her. "Sorry."

"Should we...do you need to stop?"

"No. Do you?"

This time she's the one who laughs. I honestly don't get how she can be so nonchalant, when that kiss did something to me. I thump a fist to my sternum.

"No, last night was...everything I'd never imagined it would be."

"So, it was good? Helpful?"

"I'm not scoring you on your lessons, you know, Professor, this is more of a—"

She stops dead, probably at the look on my face. Or maybe it's the choked sound I made. Because, fuck, there it is again. The feeling that this sweet, inexperienced woman might be as dirty as they come.

And, Christ, I want to explore that with her.

"What?"

I clear my throat. "Nothing."

After a beat, she seems to come to a decision. "Okay." She indicates the food. "Should we eat?"

I look around. "Want to watch something?"

"Oh. Like a show?"

"Or a movie, maybe?"

"Let me get my laptop." She runs upstairs, giving me a perfect view of her ass. It's round and pert, wider at the hips. I swear my mouth waters.

By the time she's back, I've torn into my pizza, just for something to do with my hands. And my mouth.

She sets up the computer and we scroll through the possibilities.

"You got a favorite movie, Jerusha?"

"Oh. Not yet. But I'm working on it."

"What do you mean?"

"Everybody's got favorites, but I didn't watch stuff growing up, so there's lots of catching up to do. I want a favorite, too." She settles on the floor again and I scoot closer. "What about you?"

"Do I have favorites? When I was a kid, it was war movies. *Full Metal Jacket, Platoon. Deer Hunter.*"

"I haven't seen any of those."

"They're dark and violent."

"And you watched them as a child?"

"Yeah." I shrug. "Nobody gave a crap what I did. Worst fight I ever got in with Harper's mom was when I came home after closing one night to find her still up, watching some shitty action movie. She was like five."

"Oh no."

"Anyway, when I was young, I liked that stuff and I really loved *The Matrix.* That was a favorite for a while. Today, I don't know. Maybe *Inception? Interstellar?* Something with twists and turns. A mystery, I guess."

"That sounds fun!" She hits one key. "*Indiana Jones and...the Raiders of the Lost Ark?*"

"How'd you get that from..." I squint at the screen and see that she's put an I in the search bar. "Movies starting with I? Seriously?"

"Yeah. I mean, that's what your recent favorites had in common. Makes sense, right?"

I lean forward and kiss her again, briefly. Just a peck, but her lips cling and it goes on until birdsong and music and voices break in. The movie's started. "You staying down there?" I ask.

"I like eating on the floor."

"Okay, then." I shift and slide in beside her—a tight fit under the coffee table, but it's nice being close to her. And, if we're doing this pretend date thing, it might as well be realistic. I lift my beer, with a quick cheers before putting it to my lips.

"Oh. Wait." She raises her glass. "To heavy petting," she says with the cutest smile I ever saw.

Fuck me, do I enjoy corrupting her.

14

CAN'T STOP

JERUSHA

Pizza and a movie isn't at all what I imagined for tonight.

I guess I'd pictured us getting straight to the heavy petting, which, from everything Alba and Mikey told me, is one of the crowning glories of...what did they call it? *Carnal Knowledge.* Granted, they laughed when they called it that, but still, I kind of like the term. It's somehow both Biblical and dirty.

I cover my excitement with a bite of pizza and a sip of red wine, staring at the screen, which features men in a South American jungle.

I follow the action, although every ounce of my awareness is inside this room. After a few moments, I narrow my focus on the movie. "This is kind of old."

Karl snorts. "That a problem?"

"Nope." I bite into my pizza, pretending to watch.

He shifts, bringing our thighs together. I take another bite, another. If someone ever asks me what this film's about, I'll have no idea what to tell them.

Maybe ten minutes later, he sets down his empty beer and

turns slightly toward me. "Mind if we sit on the sofa now? Back's killing me."

"Oh, sure. Sorry."

He grunts and gets up, settling into the corner of the sofa. "C'mere."

I glance at his face before sliding into the curve of his arm and what I see there sends a rush of anticipation through me. "Is this... Are we...?"

"This is good. Relax." He wraps his arm around me.

I've never felt so small. In a good way.

"Here." He urges my legs over his lap, so I'm half on him, sort of cradled. If I turn left, I'm facing the screen, to the right is his chest.

I resist the pull and force myself to watch. His hand rubs my arm up and down in a slow, even rhythm.

When his knuckles graze my breast, I'm as startled as a rabbit. He barely notices. His only response is to tighten his hold, pulling me closer to him. I don't realize right away that he's hard under my leg, but when I do, it's all I can think about.

No, that's not true. There's that hand, which has gone from the occasional accidental touch to a deliberate stroke. The side of my breast tingles, my nipples harden into painful points. But when I turn to look at him, he's clearly engrossed in what we're watching. His eyes meet mine. "You okay? Like it?" One eyebrow goes up. "The movie, I mean?"

I nod.

"Good." His eyes slide away from mine. "Keep watching." His voice is ominously deep. A daddy voice, I'll bet my friends would call it.

What feels like ages later, he shifts again. This time, his right hand slides between my legs, to my calf, and slowly up. I let out a sound—more grunt than language. In response, he lifts his hips. He's undeniably hard.

And I'm undeniably wet.

"Are we..." I turn to press my face just below his neck. "Pretending we're not doing this?"

He bends. "You like it?"

At my nod, he leans back again, spreads out his body, taking up more space on this sofa than any single person should. The wide-open pose is arrogant and casual. I have no idea why that turns me on, but it does. I'm all squirmy inside.

And then my brain catches up to my body with a rush of understanding, and I *get* it. Everything Mikey and Alba talked about makes sense in a way it didn't before.

His hand twists between my legs, making space there the way he's done on my couch. In my life. My knees fall inexorably open.

His hot palm on my sex forces my eyes shut. I don't make a sound.

He does, though. He grunts, with something like satisfaction though when I turn unfocused eyes from the screen, nothing about his position has changed. If anything, he looks even more relaxed and comfortable than before, almost lazy, I'd say, if it weren't for the ticking in his jaw.

It's heady to take him in up close like this. And it's not just his size, though he's so much bigger than me, but the details that I've only been able to admire from afar—thick black stubble, with the occasional silvery glint, the strong bump of his Adam's apple, the hair peeking out from the unbuttoned V-neck of his long-sleeved cotton T-shirt. These details, maybe more than anything we've done, make this whole thing feel real. Slowly, so as not to somehow break the unspoken rules, I let my head fall against his chest.

Barely breathing, I soak it up: the slow thump of his heartbeat against my ear, the primitive smell of him, sexy and indescribable, and there—oh, God, *there*—the insistent press of his fingers between my legs.

I catch sight of them and gasp. His hand is huge. Those fingers wide and thick. Yes, I've seen them before, but I've never seen them working my body, never pictured them stretching me open, the way he promised—*threatened*—last night.

He has to know how worked up I am, but he ignores it, like it's no concern of his. He'll do things in his own sweet time.

At this point, I'd give *anything* to take things farther. He doesn't even have to ask. He can do what he wants, sitting there, massive and full of himself and in-charge. Pure daddy.

By the time he sets me away from him, I'm so caught up in the reality blurring into the fantasy that I'm his.

He lifts his chin, eyes still glued to the screen. "Close the curtains."

I jump to comply, on a spring, too turned on to be embarrassed by my eagerness, or annoyed that he's making me do it.

"Take off your pants," he says, the way he'd order a coffee.

"Okay," I whisper, my mouth clamping down before the *Daddy* can escape.

"Good." He sprawls, legs and arms wider, and watches me through slitted eyes. I've no idea what he thinks of my best blue underwear—plain, but pretty—my soft belly, my trembling thighs. "Sit on me."

"Uh. Oh, sure." I move to do it, face-to-face, but he stops me with a curt head shake and a firm hand on my hip.

"Other way."

I'm bubbling up with nerves when I settle on his lap. His arm captures my chest, drawing my top half to him, while his other hand spreads my legs open, pressing them wide, against his. I'm his rag doll.

"Good." He pats my knee. "Very good."

My legs try to shut of their own accord, to squeeze all the pleasure I can from his words and touch, his crude, demanding presence.

He won't let me move, though, won't let me be anything but his tool. Or his student, I guess. Or something else that I can't quite grasp.

Oh, but isn't that a lie? Because, yes, I understand it. I get it on a cell-deep level and this *thing* explains why he's the one I want, the *only* one who can be this for me.

With a low warning growl, he scrubs his gruff hand up my inner thigh and my brain shorts out, leaving nothing but the knowledge that, finally, it's happening.

Daddy's home.

Karl

I'm a terrible mentor, way too into it. Way too selfish. I should fire myself.

Not gonna happen, though. Not when she's warm and willing, wriggling in my lap. Not when her breathing's gone all wild again, like last night, only right fucking here. Not when I can smell that sweet pussy in the air and, soon, so damn soon, on my fingers.

I'm drawing this out for her, but if I had my way, I'd be back against the couch cushions with her right where I need her— sitting on my face.

This torture's good, although I can't say who's learning the lessons here; her with my hands on her body, or me, holding myself back, cock pounding like a pulse in my brain.

"Good," I whisper, feeling so pervy and sick and fucking loving every second. "Good."

My finger hits the edge of those cute panties and even breathing's a chore—something I have to consciously think about, while every essential brain cell rushes south.

"Gonna touch your pussy," I whisper in her ear. "You want that?"

"Oh, yes. Yes." The words are shaky and breathy and I love that, too. Christ, I love the way her whole body's trembling.

Slower than syrup, I let my finger trace the thin cotton. My eyes slam shut as I outline the dips and rises of her feminine flesh. Even though I stared at the screen, Indiana Jones disappeared from my consciousness ages ago, but suddenly the voices are back —dudes yelling something, vague and excitable. It's a weird soundtrack to what's happening here.

Her mound's so plump, I can't help but squeeze it. Her response—a gratifying grunt—makes me do it again, and again, when she arches back, driving her head into my shoulder.

"Good." My hand pulls away long enough to make her squirm for more. "Shhhhh." I press into the side of her face and then—fuck I can't stop—I slap her cunt, light and quick.

She's writhing now, her body alive and hungry, while she expels a low, constant moan. It's so honest and open and real that I lose a part of myself.

Another shushing does nothing to quiet her, but I continue the charade. For her? For me? In the name of all that is horny and filthy and wrong in the world, I take in the wet spot on her plain little panties and tut, like some goddamn professor.

Like I'm her mentor for real and I'm disappointed at her brazen responses, when we both know—hell the family living next door must know by now—that I'm eating this up.

At this point, it'll take a fire to stop me from sliding my fingers beneath the fabric and, when I do... Ah, hell. That first touch of dry skin to slick pussy shoots my blood pressure sky high. All I can do is slide between her slippery lips and ride it out, my chest contracting like a bellows, my breath a storm in my ears.

"You're fucking soaked." My left arm lets her go to pull the panties aside for my hungry right hand.

"I know, Da—" She gulps and stops moving.

I freeze.

"What's that?" I say, aiming for light. It comes out rough and grim.

"I..." Shaky exhale "I know."

"The other word. The one you started to say."

"I..."

"Say it." My left hand grips her soft pubic hair, eliciting a gasp that lifts her tits and presses her ass to my cock even harder than before. "Say it, Jerusha. Say the word."

"It's... I don't know if—"

I open my mouth, ready to beg.

"Daddy." Her whisper's so low I could almost be mistaken, but my dick knows what it heard.

I tighten my grip, bowing her body, lifting her hips from my lap, while my other hand slides down her creamy slit. "Say that again." I circle her entrance and let my knuckles ease back up to where her clit's pulsing, hard and sweet and eager.

"Yes, Daddy."

"Fuck." I flick her clit, edge my fingers down and let a thick knuckle penetrate her, my control hanging by a thread. "*Fuck!*"

She grinds, I thrust, my hands plaster her against me.

Another circuit has us groaning together. Up, around her clit, down to tease her entrance. This time, I slide the tip of my finger inside.

Silence, broken by yelling and music from the movie, and a raw chorus of raspy exhalations. "Good," I whisper, my penetration painfully unhurried. "Just take it. Take it."

A slow in, a leisurely out, a second finger, so tight it's already a stretch. "You ever taste yourself?"

"N-no."

"Here." I pull my hand away and press my finger to her bottom lip, shiver when she hesitates. She laps up her own juices, and I go back for more. "This one's for me." Fucking into her is so much lewder when it's for the sole purpose of tasting, drawing a sample for my own pleasure. I suck my fingers and her taste's everything I've wished for. Musky, salty-sweet desire.

I try to say something, but all that emerges is a low, grumbling sound of satisfaction and then with a bitten-out, "Fuck it," I dive into motion, my body taking over from what's left of my brain.

"C'mere." I lie down on the sofa and lift her up and over, so that one dimpled leg's stretched to the floor, while the other's bent at the knee. "Sit on me."

I look up and there it is—like the holy grail—her juicy, pink cunt.

"Got to eat you," I warn before pulling her ass cheeks apart, yanking her down and plastering her pussy to my face.

15

JUST CAN'T GET ENOUGH

JERUSHA

Nothing Alba or Mikey said could have prepared me for the way Karl consumes me, like he's starving and he can't get enough.

For a few seconds, I float above him not knowing which way to go or look, my hands suspended in the air. But then his tongue runs up me, while his hands pull me in the other direction, and I fall forward with an unholy shriek, hands landing on the sofa arm.

His only response is to grunt and keep going. Up and down and around and kissing me, there, like it's my mouth. Only lewder. My goodness, so lewd I'm a little shocked.

I grip onto the couch fabric, shut my eyes and just feel. Tongue and lips, soft beard, rough five o'clock shadow. Oh! His nose and, there, my God, he's licking my...oh...his tongue's pressing into me, his teeth nip, his mouth opens wide enough to devour, and all the while he's snarling, reminding me of some wild beast with a fresh catch.

I gasp as he lifts me and moves me up, then tight to him, his mouth suctioning my clitoris, tongue flicking fast.

I open my eyes in time to catch his dark, dangerous gaze, and we both go still.

There's a distinct savagery between us—mostly him, but a bit me—and this moment encapsulates it. Like a big cat with his prey, his fierce eyes hold mine tighter than the grip on my bottom.

Slowly, I open one hand and let it skim over his sweat-beaded forehead, angry brows, and flushed cheek to the glistening curve of his mouth. He's feral, but so beautiful that my heart aches as his lips pull at my fingertip, licking it the way he licked me down there. In this moment, it's impossible to tell who's in charge—the tame girl or the beast.

I'm on top, after all, but a quick, bossy squeeze of his hands reminds me of how strong he is.

Physically, at least.

In this quiet moment, I understand something I'd never realized before. *I am strong as hell.*

Biting my lip, I circle my hips and watch his eyes roll back into his head. He's having trouble breathing and it's only partly because I'm sitting on his chest.

"You okay, Karl?" I ask, my tone almost teasing.

"Fucking love this, Jerusha."

"I..." A smirk tightens my lips. "I can tell."

"You like me eating your pussy?"

"Yes." My mouth widens into an all-out grin. And then, just to tweak him, maybe mess with our dynamic, I test this brash confidence, move my hand to his hair, and tug. "Better get back to it...Daddy."

His sigh is a thing of beauty. Unrestrained, unselfconscious, with a hint of frenzy beneath it all. It's that and his expression, almost more than the contact, that sends me toward climax. I'm sailing, close enough to feel its singe, when his eyes return to mine. The connection, in that moment, isn't just potent, it's soul-shattering.

And that's how I come, snared by the world's deepest gaze—

twin black holes sucking and spitting me out into the universe. Just another star. Just another sun glowing big and bright and too hot to last.

Karl

Her face shows me everything.

Joy and satisfaction and gratifying surprise. Which, yeah, I suck it up, knowing damn well that she's never come this hard in her life.

As she comes down, she shows tender emotions that shouldn't be there.

Not now, between the older mentor and the woman who's just figuring things out.

She should save this for the guy she winds up with. The one who'll give her love and babies and whatever it is she's looking for.

Not me.

I loosen my hold, saddened when her hand goes lax, releasing my hair. She's heavier now, and I like the way her body's not bothering to lift up.

She *can't* with the orgasm I just gave her. Pride edges out the other stuff, along with possessiveness at her hot cheeks and hazy eyes. She hasn't caught her breath yet.

It's her climax, but it's mine, too. I gave it to her, made her take it.

"Your first one," I say, watching her face with every ounce of my attention. "With a man."

Her nod's this languid thing, her body sinuous. With one lazy arm, she shoves her cloud of hair from her face and finally focuses on me.

"Crushing you."

"I like it." I give her ass a smack, jolting us both. When she seems like she'll climb off, I urge her back instead, enjoying the slow slide of her cunt all the way to my chest, and further. If only I'd thought to undress, she'd be bathing me in her come right now. I can't stop my cock from twitching at the thought. And she's right there to feel it. She lifts her head and squints down at me.

"How'd you do that?"

I play dumb. "What?"

"Move your..."

"My cock?"

Her teeth sink into her bottom lip and those pupils dilate so far, I should be able to see my reflection. "Yeah."

"When I'm really turned on, it sort of pulses. Like it wants to get in you." I narrow my eyes. "You want it in you?"

She gasps.

"Not tonight," I hurry before she gives an answer I might not like. "Next lesson."

"Yes." Heavy lidded like this, she looks older and somehow knowledgeable. Like she's done this before. Like she's the one calling the shots. It's confirmed when she reaches so low I'm sure she'll cup my erection. Disappointment cramps my belly when she moves, tugging my shirt up instead to put her hand on my hip. I want this position, only her, skin to skin. Just her and me, plastered so close we've got to be pried apart.

She rolls to her side and explores my belly, my side, brushing the shirt up to drag her fingers through my chest hair, before teasing circles around one nipple. When I think she'll move off again, I clamp my hand to hers, keeping her here.

Out of breath, I pull back. "I want your mouth."

Questions cycle over her face. *Where?* she asks herself and I want the answer so fucking badly. She surprises me, when, instead of bending forward to kiss my lips like I picture, she runs her tongue over that pebbled nipple, sending sparks through me.

"You're bossy," she says, between licks.

"I am."

"I like it."

"Good." I make a happy sound as she moves to the other side. "Take off your shirt."

She sits up to straddle me, gets rid of her shirt, and watches me watch her, eyes intense. "I'm wondering, though."

My hands are an inch from her lush, round breasts when she clasps my wrists to stop them.

"Huh?" Takes a second to focus on what she's saying.

Slowly, she dips, laps at my lips, and rises again. "Nothing."

With my hands imprisoned and her tits out of reach, every muscle's straining to get more of her. But she's owning me, turning the tables.

Shit, I'm breathing hard, like I've run up a mountain.

"Tell me," I demand, the second she sits up again, taking her body away from me. She's fiendish, suddenly, controlling in a way I'd never imagined and, fuck, but I like it. "Move up."

"Hmmm?" She circles her hips again. The hard friction of her cunt to my cock is painfully good.

"Put your pussy on my belly. So I can feel..."

I groan when she complies.

"Goddamn, you're so fucking hot."

"I feel hot."

"Yeah. On fire."

"You're burning, too." She lets one of my hands go and my brain doesn't have to give orders—I'm already squeezing and weighing her, already dipping into the plain stretchy cotton of her bra. A sedate dark blue, some logical place in my brain recognizes, just before my fingers reach their goal. I grab her and shuttle up to sitting.

With a surprised yelp, she clings to me, bringing things back into balance—our crotches line up, our bodies nested together. Her little bout of control's pushed me far, though. There's no restraint when I yank the cups down, fold myself in half, intent on taking one round nipple in my mouth, and then pause.

"Pink," I grate out. "Knew it."

And then I'm on her, licking and nipping and sucking her deep. What I'm saying's unintelligible, a drawn-out song. Like howling.

Which is exactly how I feel right now—I'm a beast, baying at the moon, expressing...goddamnn it, *ownership*.

I bite her, just a little. Just to show her.

Her panting eggs me on.

The other nipple, then a nibbled path over chest and collarbone to her neck, where I clamp on as gently as I can, while my hands... Shit, they're grasping her hips, rocking her hard, pressing, shoving dragging her down to meet every thrust I give.

I'm out of my mind. And she's done this.

When I let go, there's a bite mark there. There'll be guilt when I come back to my senses, but for now, I just lick it, suckle higher, then pull back to look at where her cunt's rubbed a wet spot on my jeans.

"Look," I mutter. "Look at how worked up you are."

"Yeah."

Foreheads together, we watch this show of our own creation. Our combined scents and sounds make this the most obscene peep show I've ever seen. But I want more. I need more.

Keeping one arm wrapped around her, I reach down and slide my fingers between us. Her reaction is electric. "Fuck, your little pussy. Fuck it's so gorgeous."

"It is?"

"Yeah. Look."

"I want..."

"What, dirty girl?" I flick her clit, teasing her into wordless, graceless grunts that'll be the soundtrack to every jerk session until the day I die.

"I want to see you, too. Touch you."

"Ooooh, fuck. I don't know."

She slows her thrusts, reminding me that I'm not always the one in charge, meets my eyes, and reaches down to my zipper, waiting. At my nod, she tugs at my button and undoes my belt.

I feel out of my mind, out of my skin, with anticipation. And then—Christ—then her cool little hands are on me. It's not until I look up and meet her gaze that I realize just how much she's turned the tables, tipped the scales, and left me inside out.

I've never felt this way. It scares the shit out of me.

16

SO YOU THINK YOU'RE IN LOVE

JERUSHA

"Oh, Karl." *It's gorgeous*, I almost whisper, though I'm pretty sure he wouldn't know what to do with that. Instead, I let him hear the awe in my breathing, see it on my face, feel it in the way I hold him.

So much has happened here tonight that a part of me wants to stop and breathe, give us—okay *me*—time to adjust, but I'm afraid if we don't do this now, I won't get another chance.

I swallow, unwilling to even think about that right now, when everything is so right.

Instead of worrying about what-ifs, I let my senses guide me, let my hands enjoy how warm and solid and smooth/soft he is. I want to lean down and kiss him there so badly, but drawing it out feels better. This way, I can memorize every step, in case this is it.

He's thick—though my only reference is the porn that I've glommed in the last few months. There's a vein along one side, reminding me of his vitality, throbbing with life and blood, strength, but also scarily close to the surface. Vulnerable.

I take a second to listen to the way his breathing changes—

almost wheezing when I tighten my grip on his crown, then drawing out into long, shaky gasps when I stroke farther down his shaft. With his jeans barely open and my body blocking the view, I can't see lower.

Yet.

"Fuck, Jerusha." His whisper's tight, restrained. I wonder, suddenly, what he's like when he really lets go.

It's almost scary, the thought of all those muscles, all the flesh and blood and bone working above me, alongside me...in me.

I shudder and loosen my grip. He takes advantage of that weakness to move me off his lap and onto the sofa. I watch, obscenely half-naked with my bottom half nude and my breasts spilling over my bra. I like how crude it makes me feel...

I'm a slut. For him.

Under my stare, he stands and pulls his shirt the rest of the way off, then drags his pants off entirely. I lap up the show. *This could be the last time* is my tragic inner anthem.

There's no time for me to think before he's kicked off his pants and climbed back on top, his underwear still in place. It's an interesting decision, but I like it, the way I like still wearing my bra. Fantasies rush in as he stretches out on top—us in his restaurant office, against the door, only this time, he pulls himself from his underwear, tugs mine to the side and shoves that fat cock inside me.

I moan at the reel in my head, and at the heavy bulk of him, pinning me in place as solidly as his hungry gaze.

He rises up onto straightened arms, giving me space to breathe. I'm still taking him in, memorizing every square inch of this powerful body. His ink, his scars, the rippling muscles I'd only guessed at.

"You okay?" he asks, concern diluting his desire.

"Oh, yes." I nod. "You?"

He dips his hips, rubbing his cotton-clad erection between my splayed thighs.

I whimper. He grins evilly. The balance is restored.

"I'm good." He lifts up again, clears his throat. "As long as this is what you want and you don't—"

"It is," I rush to say. "I want this." *I want you.*

His gaze sharpens as it skims over my face, like he's considering, after everything, if maybe we're about to go too far.

We're not! I want to scream. *Do it. Do it all, Karl. Do it, Daddy.*

Instead I watch him with steady eyes, hoping he can't feel the wild tripping of my heart, only partially in reaction to his hard penis. Most of it, though, I have to attribute to *him* and my feelings. Which was not part of the deal.

"Come on, Daddy," I whisper, as flirtatiously as I can. "I want to feel you down there."

His eyes lose focus as he groans and gives in, dipping low, with nothing but underwear between us.

Back and forth, he strokes, the pressure wonderful, but the fabric not ideal. It doesn't take long for my hands to roam, raking through his coarse hair before stroking his flank. His belly's hard abs ripple when I reach down to skim him there.

His rhythm is measured until I reach around to his butt, tuck my fingers in his boxer briefs, and tug.

"I want you bare. Against me," I venture, hoping I'm not going too far.

"Oh, fuck, you're so dirty." With his weight on one arm, he wrenches the shorts partway down. I help him, tugging until they're almost to his knees. Without the fabric's restraint, his cock strains up to his belly. He amends that with a quick, downward tug and then—

I'm sunk, swimming in sensation.

All I feel is his heat, his hardness. It's so much more than I imagined. So real it's a little frightening.

Being me, though, the fear ramps things up, makes my

nipples point so high they hurt. I can smell myself and him and the cocktail of our bodies together and it's absolutely magic.

"That's it, use me. Use it," he mutters.

I'm so wet he slides right between my lips. We both jump like live wires, as if our nerves are centered right where our bodies meet.

His butt flexes under my hand, full of power. The potential makes me go weak. If he shifts, just enough, he'll be in me, breaching me for the first time.

"I want you to do it, Karl. I want you inside me."

"Yeah," he mumbles, drawing back, his eyes glued to where so much is happening. "Yeah, I'll fuck you so hard."

"You seem big. Are you... Are you sure?"

He slows his back and forth motion, narrows his eyes. "Sure of what?"

"That you'll fit?"

His sordid chuckle sends a fresh wave of lust from my core to my limbs. Recklessness takes over.

"I'll fuck you. Don't you worry," he threatens. "I'll stretch that tight little cunt and you'll take it. You'll take what I give."

"Oh, gosh." As soon as I say it, the word sounds silly mixed with the sex in the air. I stutter out a broken *yes.*

"Say my name."

"Karl."

"That's right."

"I'll take it, Karl. I want that."

"Good."

The talk from last night, but face-to-face, skin to skin, flips every switch. The heat's almost unbearable. The pressure too much to take. His shaft presses and slides, his ass clenches, his arms so tense that they're shaking and all of it—every little twitch, every bit of effort—is for me. For *me.*

He rears back, face taut and deadly serious, rubs my clit hard and fast.

I catch fire, incapable of holding the orgasm back. It barrels through me, tears away every bit of restraint I have, blasts straight to my heart.

I love him, I admit, soaking up his expressions of mixed pleasure and pain. I love him and I don't ever want this to end.

It's too much. I'm not breathing, not moving. I swear even my heart goes still.

But my mouth, crap, my mouth says the words. "I love you, Karl."

So I guess that's that.

Karl

I love you, Karl.

No. God, don't say that.

My vision blurs and her hand lands on mine to stop the friction. Watching her features freeze and her face go beautifully blank with pleasure, I want to do it again, give her another orgasm and another; force them on her 'til she forgets what she just said. Or maybe I'm the one who needs to forget.

Fuck. I shove her words out of my head, lean back, and wrap my fist around my dick, work it hard until coming's an inevitability. All thoughts of feelings and futures and responsibilities scatter. I picture doing it on her belly, her tits. Anywhere. Inside her. I want to rub it in. Bite her, mark her. Own her.

No dammit.

I love you, Karl.

I pull away, chest hurting. Okay. Okay. She came. Lesson over.

I look up. On the computer, the credits are rolling. I should go. Give her some space, let her get to sleep.

"You good?" I ask, yanking my underwear over my aching erection. I step back, knock into the table, which tips my beer bottle. I save the computer, but beer spills everywhere. Laptop in one hand, I grab the first thing I find—my shirt—and sop the foam up, trip on my jeans, and finally sit back down on the sofa. "*Dammit.*"

The look on Jerusha's face is half-shock, half-hilarity. None of the lazy, post-orgasmic glow she should be wearing. She's wrapped her arms around her legs and sits in a tight ball in the corner of the couch.

"Here." She reaches out. "Let me take that."

I hand over the laptop, watch her set it down on a side table—calm and cool—and let my head fall into my hands. "Sorry."

"No. No, that was...*amazing.*" She's laughing.

"Which part? The orgasm or the after-show?"

She smirks. "A little of both."

I make an attempt at a laugh. "Sorry, it's uh...getting late."

"Yep." Her expression loses its humor.

"I'll let you get some sleep."

Eyes steady on mine, she nods. "Sure. Sounds good."

"All right." I stand up again, slip on my damp shirt with a grimace, and finish getting dressed, while Jerusha does the same. "Look, ah, Jerusha. This is probably a good time to stop the lessons."

She exhales. "Right."

"You've got the basics now." I shrug into my jacket, feeling as foolish as I ever have. Basics? Lessons? What a dick. "You're free to..."

"Use what I've learned with someone else. Got it."

My hands tighten into fists. "Great." I stalk to the door, step into the cold and turn. Backlit in the doorway, wrapped in a blanket, she's so fucking pretty it makes my chest hurt. Too young. Too giving, too innocent. Too big of a future to fuck it up with a guy twice her age.

I open my mouth, to tell her... What? That she doesn't want an asshole like me hanging around? And there's no way what she feels is love. It's gotta be the orgasm talking. Jesus, what would she want with me anyway? I can't love her back. I can't give her the life she deserves.

"Night, Jerusha."

"Good night, Karl."

I head down her porch steps, feet leaden. Her door closes before my boots hit the sidewalk.

Good. Now, she can forget tonight's delusion and we'll go back to just being neighbors.

17

HEAVEN KNOWS I'M MISERABLE NOW

JERUSHA

"You told him *what?*"

"Shhhhhh!" I glance around our coffee shop, suddenly paranoid that Karl or Harper or someone from the university will show up and hear everything I'm whispering to my friends. Every sad little detail of what could have been the most amazing night ever. "I told him I love him."

"*Why?*" Alba is clearly aghast.

"Because I do."

Mikey groans, dropping their head on their folded arms. After a too-long stretch of what I'm supposed to perceive as agony, they lift their head and give me an annoyed look. "That's not how you do it with guys like that."

"Guys like what?"

"Big, alpha, you know..." Alba looks to Mikey for help.

Fluttering their hands, Mikey finishes. "Macho, *macho* men. Strong, silent types."

"I don't..." I shake my head, feeling more lost than I have

since I moved here. I could cry right now. All night, the tears built up in my sinuses, my chest. One overly kind word from these two and the dam will break.

The coffee shop's packed, the music loud, the conversation constant. We're at our usual corner table. At the next table over, two women are showing each other pictures on their phones. I can't hear them, which I hope means they can't hear us either. The air is full of spices and steamed milk and some herbal scent Mikey's wearing. All things that usually buoy my spirits.

"You two are speaking a foreign language to me right now. I mean, I grew up with people who never talked about themselves. So, I get that it's a thing. It's just..." I look around for inspiration, but see none. Everything's sort of dark today, colorless. "He's not silent. He talks to me. We talk."

"About sex? Work? Sure." Alba's wearing an almost pained expression. "But not love."

"Love's taboo, honey."

"What?" My face squishes up. "I thought the dad—" Remembering where we are, I whisper, "I thought the daddy thing was taboo. And my wanting to be submissive. I get that about spankings and role play and whatever, but now you're telling me *love* is? Feelings? Emotions?"

"No, no, no. Not taboo, like sexually," Mikey says. "Big Daddy Karl seems to be perfectly fine with pushing those limits."

Alba nods her confirmation, full lips pursed.

"It's..." Mikey lets out a slow, exhausted raspberry. "Okay. So. The white American cishet male is afraid."

I blink, picturing Karl's face when he kicked that man out of his bar. I see the breadth of his shoulders and the strength in those hands. No fear. At all. "He's scared of nothing."

"He's afraid of *you*."

"That's absurd." Frustration pushes me to stand. "This is ridiculous. I'm not asking him for *anything!*"

"You want him to love you back." Mikey puts out a hand and wraps it around mine. Theirs is warm and dry and strong. Comforting. "Right?"

"It would be nice, but... No." I sink down and give their hand a squeeze. Alba takes hold of my other one. "Maybe."

"Give him time."

I grimace. "I get impatient."

"You do," Alba says with a smirk.

I tighten my hold on them before extricating my hands and sip my coffee for a quiet moment, letting the taste and smells lift me up again. I wrap my favorite scarf around my neck. The fact is, whatever happens, however this thing pans out, I'll do it on my terms. That's important.

I picture him, last night, hands on me, face on me. I remember the way our bodies worked together, and the feel of him, so hefty, so strong and *hot*. The way our connection created an energy of its own. I want that again. I want more. "I think of all the stuff we didn't get to do."

"Stuff?"

"Blow jobs? Intercourse?" The women beside us are openly listening now. I blush, hard, and roll my eyes theatrically in their direction.

With an impish grin, Alba stage-whispers, "Don't forget anal!"

I shush her, laughing, despite my discomfort. "You're a nightmare."

"I know. I know."

Beside us, the women rise and head to the door, heads close together, maybe scandalized or excited or a bit of both. Or, given the general volume in here, they're probably talking about something completely unrelated to our discussion. I watch them push outside and link arms to stroll down the crowded sidewalk.

What would that be like? Walking with someone like Karl.

Maybe holding hands, just casually, as we head off to dinner or something.

From out of nowhere, Karl's words from the night before come back to me. *Look, ah, Jerusha. This is probably a good time to stop the lessons.*

Mikey squints. "What? What just happened? What are you thinking about?"

"He wants to stop the lessons."

"He said this? After the *I love you?*"

I nod.

"No. Hell, no." Alba's got that hard-eyed look she gets when something displeases her. "Y'all have too much chemistry. This thing isn't over."

I'm not sure I believe that, but I nod, swallowing back the fear that I've done something I can't fix. Something wrong. My eyes land on my hands, which are rough and callused, scarred and stained. More like Karl's than Mikey's slender, soft ones or Alba's plump, dimpled, manicured ones.

My hands are good hands. *Strong* hands. I suck in a breath full of that strength and face my friends. "I didn't do anything wrong by telling him."

They shake their heads.

"No, honey, you didn't." Mikey leans in. "You were just being...you."

"And you are fucking *perfection.*"

Someone clears their throat, interrupting my snort-laugh.

I look up into Harper's blushing face. "Oh, hi!" is all I manage.

Judging from Mikey's slow grin, they're happy to see her. Harper, however, is all wide-eyed insecurity. That's new.

"Hey, Harper," says Alba.

"Am I interrupting something?"

"We were just talking about your dad." I'd get mad, except Alba's grin is so flat-out happy, I can't.

"But we're done," I say, shaking my head as I stand to give Harper my chair. "Have a seat."

She flops down with the kind of easy, long-limbed grace that I envied when I was younger. I don't anymore. I like myself, my body. My strong bits and my soft bits and the way I am inside. I *like* that I love Karl, because it's open and it's honest and that's who I am.

Dammit. *That's* who I am.

I take a deep breath and button my jacket, pretending like Harper's not the daughter of the man I professed to love just a few days ago. The man I love. "Have fun, you guys."

"Oh, we will," replies Mikey with a smirk. "You, too, honeybear."

I roll my eyes, grab my bag, and take off for the door.

Karl

I can't stop thinking about Jerusha. And not just thinking, but aching, like my body's already addicted and it needs her. My chest, my belly, my balls.

Did I have to cancel the goddamn lessons?

Yes. Yes, I had to. For *her*. I did it to give her a life. A chance at a real future, instead of an unhealthy attachment to the first guy who got her off.

But, shit. The four days since that night have felt like a goddamn month. I shouldn't even be at the bar tonight, but I couldn't sit at home one more fucking minute. Instead, I'm getting in the way, polishing glasses, prepping mixers, hauling a fresh keg out of the back. I've counted the till out three times, distracted as hell.

I know I've annoyed the crap out of the bartender. She said something about making shrub and disappeared into the kitchen half an hour ago. When I slipped in there in search of prep work, my chef ordered me out.

My phone vibrates and I practically rip off my pocket yanking it out. It's a number I don't recognize.

"Hello?"

"Mr. McCoy? This is Andy Gentry from Virginia First."

My pulse returns to normal while the banker tells me the good news. My loan's been approved.

As of this time next week, I'll be sole owner of this place. I hang up feeling lighter. I automatically open my texts before remembering that I'm not supposed to contact Jerusha. My rule.

We need space. Both of us, to get back to our regular lives.

I can't help but wonder how she managed, in such a short time, to become the first person I want to share news with.

"Harper," I slip out from behind the bar as my daughter walks by with a tray full of roll-ups. "Come here."

"No. No, way, dude."

"What? Don't want the good news?"

"Good news? Dad. You look like someone *died*. I need this..." She waves a circle in my direction, her expression exactly like when she used to eat lemons as a toddler. "To clear up before I come within, like five feet of Mr. Sourpuss Poopoo Pants."

"We got the loan."

After a few blank seconds, she sets her tray on the bar and jumps up and down. "Dave the Douchebag's out?"

"A few days for the funds to come through and I'm sole owner."

She steps up on the rail and leans over to give me a hug. "We should celebrate!" When she pulls away, she's wearing a sly look. "Is there someone you'd like to celebrate with, perhaps?"

"What?"

"Oh, just your neighbor." Her eyes narrow. "No plans to see her again?"

"I... Nope." I shake my head, jaw tight. "No, that's over."

"O-kay. Sure," she says in that *whatever, Dad* tone of voice, before picking up her tray and flouncing off.

Christ. I blink at my phone screen before shoving it back into my pocket and stalking off to check garnishes. As if I haven't already done that. As if I should even be here tonight.

My mind keeps fucking with me—giving me images of her sitting at the bar, nursing a champagne. I'd pull an off-menu bottle if she were here—the pink stuff we keep for special occasions. God, she'd love that, wouldn't she? And she'd be so goddamn happy for me—for Harper, too.

I picture her, leaning forward, bright face surrounded by all that hair, her scarf trailing behind her, a hint of unintentional cleavage. My dick gets heavy just thinking about it. I remember the freckles on her collar bone—the ones I didn't get a chance to count the other night, because, dammit, I can't give her any of the shit she deserves. I can't give her a fucking thing.

"Dad."

I look up. "What?"

"Step away from the lemons."

I look down at the huge pile I've butchered. Jesus. Time to pull my head out of my ass or God only knows what other havoc I'll wreak. I'm shocked I didn't slice my hand open, especially given that I'm using one of my best knives. Definitely not a good idea in my current mood.

Harper slides behind the bar and walks up to me, looking worried. "Seriously. What's wrong?"

"I..." I huff out a breath. No way am I explaining any of what's happened to my eighteen-year-old daughter. She may be wise beyond her years, but she doesn't need to hear about the agreement I had with my neighbor. Or the fact that it's over. "I'm good."

"You are so full of shit." Her sigh's teenager-eloquent. "I know what this is about."

Shit, I hope not.

"If it's any consolation, Dad, she looks like crap, too."

"What?"

"Your..." She wags her fingers in my face. "Neighbor girlfriend."

"She's not my—"

"Oh, for God's sake, Dad. Are you seriously telling me there's nothing between you?"

"It's over."

"She broke up with you?" Her eyes narrow into angry little slits. "I will tear her a new—"

"Stop."

For once she listens. Of course, I have no idea what to say. Apparently my silence gives me away.

"You ditched her? Why?"

"She's too young."

"Oh my God."

"What?"

"You like her."

"No, it was just..." Don't say it, dickhead. "I don't know—casual. She's young. Deserves a chance at a real future and I'm not the—"

"Hold on. What? She said you're too old for her? I'll show that—"

"*Harper.* Listen. She didn't say that. *I'm* saying that."

She backs up a step, face drawn into a *you've gotta be kidding me* expression. "You ended it to *help* her?"

"Yeah." My fist tightens around the lime I don't remember picking up. I want to hurl it across the room.

"But you like her." Obviously exasperated, she yells. "Why do I keep having to remind you of that?"

"It's not—"

"You fucking *do!*" Wow. Harper's *pissed.* I have no idea why.

"Whoa. Let's not—"

"No, *let's.*" Her finger's in my face. "You broke up with the first person I've ever seen you actually *into*—and that includes Mom—because *you* think she deserves better?"

"She *does*," I say, reasonably.

"Decrees His Royal Highness Karl M. McCoy the third."

"The third? I'm not the thir—"

"Whatever. You're breaking it off because *you* know what *she* needs. That it?" Her head's shaking, mouth tight. "You know what, Dad? That's fucking stupid."

I open my mouth to reply, but she plunges on.

"Truth?" She backs up, head shaking. "I don't like that she's closer to my age than yours. It's embarrassing, okay? We have the same friends. But even I can tell that you're into her." She stomps off and then comes right back. "You'd better not be doing this for me, Dad, got it?"

I shake my head, stunned at how enraged she is.

"I know about all the stuff you gave up."

It's my turn to be mad. "What the hell are you talking about, Harper?"

"Oh, come on. I know you put me ahead of everything." She starts ticking things off on her fingers. "I know you said you were a fuck-up as a kid, but you can stop making up for it now, okay? No girlfriends, working a million jobs, extra construction hours, quitting school? You did all that crap for me."

"I'd do it again!" I'm close to yelling, myself. "Whatever it takes to make sure you have what you need. Keep you safe."

"Like sell your bike to pay for Mom's rehab?"

"She's your *mother*, Harper." I sigh, shaking my head at the memories. "You're my *kid*. It's my job to take care of you." My entire reason for being, if I'm honest. Breathing hard, I look down at my tight fists, and force them to loosen.

"Yeah? Well, Mom's good. Really good. And I'm doing pretty well." She widens her eyes and leans over the tray. I can tell whatever she's about to say is going to be a doozy. "Maybe it's time to take care of *you*, now." With that, my daughter sticks out her tongue and waltzes off, leaving me blindsided.

"Shit," I mutter, staring into space for a few seconds as what she said sinks in.

As soon as it does, I grab my jacket and head for the door.

SO WHAT'CHA WANT

JERUSHA

I finally finished my last piece for the show. I should be relieved, happy. Celebrating. All I want to do is go home and take a bath and watch some show I missed out on as a kid.

No. That's a lie. What I really want to do is text Karl and tell him *he's* missing out because there's still stuff that I haven't tried and I keep thinking about him and—

Nope. Not texting. Not calling. Not even looking to see if there's a light on in his house when I walk by. (There isn't.)

I drag myself up my steps and pull out my mail. A bill, a campaign flyer. I unlock my door, shove it open, flip to the last piece of mail, and stop.

It's a postcard. *My* postcard.

After a couple seconds, it hits me that I'm looking at one of the invitations to my big art opening and then I see that it's my parents' invitation. There's the little note from me, hand-written on the back—*Dear Mama and Papa, I really hope you can make it. It would mean the world to me. Love, Jerusha.* There's a slash through their address with the words RETURN TO SENDER scrawled in my father's handwriting. My bag thumps to the floor and all I can do is stare at the stupid thing, wondering if he wrote those words in anger or with some pious sense of superiority or if maybe, worst of all, he just doesn't care.

I should be irate. I should cry. I should call him and tell him he's a coward. Instead, I go straight upstairs to my bathroom—the one with the clawfoot tub I love so much—and strip down to nothing.

I'm about to turn the tap when someone knocks on my front door. Nobody I know comes to my house, except for...

When they knock a second time, I pull on my robe, race down the stairs, and slide the last few feet, before flipping open the lock and throwing open the door.

It's Karl.

Without warning, my face crumples.

"Jerusha, what is it? Hey. What's going on?" He reaches out and I step back, not because I don't want his touch, but because I want it way too much. "Did I hurt you? Did I make you feel this way?"

"No. Not at all." I force a smile. "I mean, I missed you, yes, but it's m-m-my dad."

"Is he okay? What do you need? I can drive you to—"

I shake my head, grab the card from the side table and hand it to him. I can tell the second he realizes what it means because his jaw hardens and his mouth goes all flat. He looks angry.

"It's no big deal. I didn't think they'd come, but I j-j-just hate that I *care*."

"Come here." His arms slide around me, pull me into that now-familiar chest, his comforting smell. It's been a few days and already, I miss this smell. "It's not okay. It's fucking not."

My chest shudders from the effort of holding the tears in.

It's pointless. My eyes are already leaking, my face pressed to his coat. I hear the door close and lock. His muscles contract and I'm no longer on the floor. I tighten my hold, though I should make him put me down. But I don't want to. I want the comfort of his arms, the solidity of these shoulders, this firm chest.

He leans down—so much bigger than I remembered—and kisses the top of my head. Just that. No words, no *Stop crying*, no *Everything's fine*. Just that kiss.

I lose it. My body's racked with painful sobs that are about so much more than a stupid returned invite. Although maybe not. That invitation wasn't just a piece of paper in the post. It was an olive branch, an open door. A chance at connection. A way of asking my family to love me, even though I don't fit into their mold.

"They don't...*want me*," I sob. "They don't love me."

He drops to the sofa in my dimly-lit living room—it's the last place Karl and I spent time together, but it might as well be another world entirely.

Even that makes me want to cry.

"I'm sorry, Karl."

He bends forward. "What?"

"I'm sorry I pressured you. I'm sorry I told you I loved—"

"No. No, Jerusha. Don't be sorry. Don't ever be sorry for how you feel. For being you."

I open my mouth to protest, maybe to tell him that being me's not working out all that well right now, but he leans down and kisses my tear-soaked mouth. Just a peck, way too small to draw a gasp from my lungs.

"*Dammit*. Come here." He shifts me so I'm straddling him, slides his fingers into my hair and cups my ears. This time when he kisses me, it's in earnest. Not a little one—a devouring of tears and hiccups and pain. Between pulls, he tilts back and looks me in the eye. "You're a force of nature." Another kiss, fierce and hard enough to bruise. "You're fucking magnificent, Jerusha." Our next kiss is lighter, more caress than consumption. "So fucking beautiful."

A disbelieving snuffle escapes me.

He tightens his hold, levers me back to stare me down with those soul-wrenching eyes. "Since you showed up, you've changed my life. Made it better. Made *me* better. Made everything so much brighter." His inhalation is as shaky as mine. "I don't..." He draws a hand from my tangled hair and smooths his knuckles over my cheek, looking at me like...like I mean something to him.

I swallow back the hope trying to creep in. It's a delusion that will only hurt me. Like the stupid invite that I should never have sent.

Karl's eyes slam shut and his forehead presses to mine. "I don't know how to... I shouldn't..."

"Shouldn't what?" I whisper.

"Be so damned selfish."

"Selfish?"

"Wanting you. It's selfish." He grunts and shakes his head. What I see of his face looks pained.

"Be selfish," I urge, surprising myself. "Be selfish with me."

He grates out another raw sound. "I don't just want your body, Jerusha. I want what you're offering. Your..." He shakes his head, jaw rock-hard. "Those looks you give me, like I'm a fucking giant? Like I could move mountains for you."

"You are. You could." I nod, my breath picking up. "I'd do the same for you, Karl. I'd do anything." I hook his arms at the elbows, and tug until his hands are in mine. I hold them tight.

"You don't know about all the shit."

I can't help but smile. "I know the *good* shit."

"Yeah? Well, I'm not all kisses and orgasms."

"I know." With a shuddering, post-cry exhale, I flip his hand over. Slowly, carefully, I pull away from him, enough to look down at the crude tattoos inked into his fingers, and over the backs of his hands. "I know you have a past. I know you have a daughter who seems pretty amazing. I know you're a good man." His gaze rakes over my face, hot as coals. "I know you hurt inside." My fingers slide between his, gripping his hand, showing him my strength. Under my bottom, I feel the hard length of him. I can't help but twist my hips, very slightly. Teasing, promising. "I want to make you feel good."

He lets out a long, slow breath and shifts almost imperceptibly beneath me. Deep in his eyes, the ferocity still burns. I want to kindle it brighter, make it hot enough to consume us both. "Will you let me do that, Karl? Let me make you feel good?" Another twist presses us tightly together, the move the most overtly sexual invitation I've ever made. "Will you let me love you?"

"I want to make *you* feel good, Jerusha. Let me take care of you tonight."

His hands move to my ass, but I've got other ideas. Slowly, confidently, despite being bright red, tear-streaked and sniffly, I settle on my knees in front of him.

His mouth drops open.

Karl

Jerusha goes to the floor between my legs and every brain cell in my body goes dormant. Or dies. I don't know. Or give a fuck.

All I care about is the hunger in her gaze, the bright color in her cheeks, the way her mouth drops open when she looks at my crotch.

I don't even notice what she's wearing until the robe slips to one side, giving me a pale, freckled shoulder. Christ, even the ugly terrycloth loves her curves, making her look like some Greek statue.

My balls have been aching for days—since the last time I sat on this couch—and the smile that curls her lips only makes it so much worse.

"Couldn't stop thinking of you," I admit, feeling raw, like I'm exposing my ugly insides. "Every second."

When she opens her mouth, I figure she'll say, *Me, too.* Commiserate, maybe. Instead, she levels me with a hard look. "Good," she says, blowing every expectation out of the water and, in the process, blowing me wide open

In that moment, I'm gone. I'm hers. I don't know if it's love, but I give in. Give up. Or the opposite. It's the moment I take up the fight, decide to *earn* her affection, to make it worth her while, to keep it no matter what it takes.

I can't get enough of this woman, with her smooth and her rough, sensitive and strong. I want to fight, to fucking obliterate whatever's in her way, to destroy anyone who hurts her.

"Now let me do this."

All I can do is swallow and nod. Follow orders. Take what she's slinging my way. Not something I've done before, but I'll give it a try. Whatever she wants.

"I *miss* the lessons, Karl. I miss talking to you. I like the way I feel with you." Sighing and shaking her head, she rises up onto her knees and reaches for my jeans. My cock throbs with anticipation. "I *want* to love you, okay? I'm not asking you to love me back. That's not what this is. This is...experience, for me. Do you get that? Loving you is a new experience. It makes me feel so good." She scans my face, looking for what, I've got no idea.

"Jerusha." I run the back of a finger down her cheek. "I—"

She stops working at my belt to slap a palm to my mouth. "Will you let me do this? After this, you can... We can... Just let me, okay? Just for tonight?"

My frustrated growl's the only response I manage.

"I've never given you an..." She bites that plump lower lip and lets her hands drop again. "Orgasm." I beg to differ, given the fantastic climax I had on the phone with her, but her expression tells me to shut up. And, fuck me, I want to do as she orders. "I want to give you a blow job, Karl."

I ignore the way my cock throbs behind my zipper and focus on what she's just said. "How do you even know that term?"

She shimmies the robe off her shoulders, giving me the view of a lifetime—her rosy cheeked, bed headed, turned-on flush, and a hint of cleavage where the robe's hanging open. I want to swipe the garment off, but she beats me to it and my mouth goes dry. I'd figured I'd never see her like this again. Relief makes me want to drop my face between her breasts and breathe her in.

"I have my ways."

"Ways?" What are we talking about?

"I know about blow jobs and...other sex stuff."

I grit my teeth when her expert hands get the belt open. "You done this before?" Like in the last four days? Jealousy stabs me right through the solar plexus, pushing me close to the edge. I feel horny, out of control, explosive.

"*Nooo.*" She gives a *duh* look, complete with eye roll. "But I've seen people doing it."

I go still. "Seen people?"

She smiles, her self-satisfied expression proving just how aware she is of her effect on me. For the first time, I wonder who's in charge here. "Mikey and Alba tell me everything." Her face wrinkles with momentary distraction. "Although not recently." She leans in. "Alba took me to a kink party."

I shake my head to clear it. "What?"

"There's also this thing called the internet. I've watched pornography."

"Porn," I repeat, dumbly aware of just how little I know her.

She shoves my legs apart, more to be bossy than because she needs to, I suspect, and unzips my jeans. "I think it's time for me to show *you*, Karl, that you don't know everything."

Her hands reach in through the slit in my shorts and pull me out. They're strong and competent, a little rough from what must be calluses on her thumbs. Feels so fucking good. I can do nothing but stare.

"And, more importantly, I know what I *want* to do." Her eyes hit mine with the impact of twin sledgehammers. "I've thought about doing this to you...a *lot*."

She leans forward and breathes on my aching cock.

My vision goes dark around the edges.

19

UNTIL SHE COMES

JERUSHA

Alba swears up and down that I talk like a sub, but I'm feeling all kinds of power right now. There's nothing subservient about the way I hold his erection and pull it toward my mouth, no docility in the directness of my gaze. Not an ounce of compliance in the gentle scrape of my teeth over the crown of his cock.

I'm toying with him, turning the tables, maybe showing *him* a thing or two.

I have no idea what I'm doing. But I *crave* this smell, this taste, these unbridled responses.

Clearly restless, he reaches out, like he's going to grab me, hesitates, then plants his hands on his knees where they remain, white-knuckled and tense.

Who's submissive now, huh?

I love those hands. I love how big and neat and square his fingertips are, I love the thick knuckles and the rough patches, the ink scrawled there like the road map of his past. I really love the dark sprinkling of hair, serving no apparent purpose but to please me. I love all of him. Every life-hardened bit.

I pull back to examine his erection closer, tighten my hold, and watch a fat, glossy drop form at his slit. "What's..."

"Precum," he bites out. "Fuck, baby, feels so good."

I lick it up, savoring the salty taste, the close-up scent. His entire body flinches, more than it did when I used my teeth, which is interesting. I lap at him in quick flicks, glance up at his face, and pause. He's riveted. Not like watching a good movie riveted, like life or death riveted.

I want more of that look.

Instead of paying attention to his sex this time, I watch *him* as I lower my head and taste him. His expression is one of pure concentration, absolute engrossment. Mayhem could break out around us, and he'd stay focused on me.

When I pause, he goes all pained. Good. I lap up that hint of suffering amidst all the pleasure. When I dip my head this time, it's to take him as far as I can. I fill my mouth and he groans like it hurts. That sound is the one I'll file away to think of when I'm touching myself later. It's uncontrolled, animalistic, wounded, and it speaks to something in my soul.

By the time I come up for breath, he's gasping and lifting his hips for more, his hands dig so deeply into his knees it's got to hurt.

I pull away and lick our combined tastes from my lips before wiping my mouth with the back of my arm. His hand twitches like he wants to yank me back. In my mind, he loses control—wraps his hand in my hair or tightens it on my throat or my breast. Maybe strokes himself while he works his big, stiff cock into my throat. My nipples zing at the idea.

"What do you need me to do?" I ask, so excited I have to squeeze my legs together.

"This. This is good."

"No. No, tell me what you like. What to do. I want something." I want him to take over.

He grunts and I can't hold back a smile. I love it. I do. I love this experience the way I love cake and adventure and the zingy scent of fall. The way I love my work and living here, on my own. And it's not just my tastebuds involved, it's my skin, my insides, my brain.

"Tell me," I whisper, feeling so much like the snake with the apple that I shiver.

"I want to..." He swallows, his eyes dashing madly over me, like he wants it all and doesn't know where to start.

"Just do it," I urge, knowing he won't hurt me.

With a narrow-eyed look, he leans close. "Suck the tip," he whispers, tangling his hands in my hair. "I'll do the rest."

Without another word, I lower my face, wrap my mouth around him, and give him back the reins.

He's gentle at first, and slow. I breathe through my nose and he pushes in. I accept, relaxing my jaw as best I can. His hands in my hair guide, without forcing, although there are moments when I wish he'd get a little rougher. But then tonight's not about that, I guess. Tonight's something else entirely.

I'll leave taking things too far for some other time.

I'm initially disappointed when he nudges me away, but when he half stands to yank down his jeans and underwear, I'm fascinated. Distracted at the way he caresses his testicles, I forget what I'm doing, but his grip on my hair brings me back in line, as effectively as the crack of a whip. My belly squirms and everything else goes haywire—my breasts, my mouth, that needy place between my legs. I reach down to relieve the ache and find myself soaking wet—no surprise.

"Oh, fuck. You touching yourself? Working that little clit? You wet for me?"

With my mouth full of cock, I can only moan my assent. He likes it, judging from the way his hips thrust. My eyes tear up, I draw back to avoid gagging, catch sight of his flushed face, and go still while he grips himself, gasping for breath. He's losing it. And it's glorious.

Though his hand's still in my hair, he doesn't force me down, he just watches me watch him. "You like this?" He strokes his shaft, the movement exaggerated, showy.

"Yeah."

"Good." Another slow, painful-looking up and down stroke, another thrust, another smooth caress of his balls. "Fuck. Your mouth... Get used to this. Taking my cock. Tasting me." His eyes rake up and down my body.

My nipples prick up, as if they know what he means, when I'm not even sure. Does he mean tonight? Does he mean for longer? "Okay."

"I need you back."

Tortuously slow, I slide my tongue down his shaft, then lower, to where that left hand's still working. With a quick glance at his face, I nudge his hand aside and lick his heavy testicles.

He goes absolutely still while I explore him. He's cooler here, his smell's sexy and potent. Curiosity and a fresh wave of desire push me to suck on him, the way I sucked his shaft, and his response is electric. Not a muscle in his body moves, as if the thread he's hanging on is too close to snapping. The only sound in the room's my hand between my legs and, when I pull slightly away from him, we're connected by my hot breath and the feel of his quiet, intense scrutiny.

Even that is a link, ephemeral, but real, like the words we exchanged on the phone. We're in this together. The pursuit of pleasure.

With our eyes joined, I lean down and drag my open mouth from testicles, all the way to the tip of his cock. That's when I suck him down again—when he least expects it and we're both weirdly vulnerable. In a flash, I give myself up, become a mess of bodily functions—spit and desire and a need to give, to get.

I go deep and suction my lips, the way the women do in the movies, then come up for air when I have to. I'm a mess of saliva and tears. His hands help me do it again, not quite *making* me lower my head, but not stopping me either, not holding me down, but showing me that he can. Maybe one day he will, if I let him. If I ask him.

For now, I'm in charge and it's heady. Growling voice, tense muscles, dark, musky scent—he's a fantasy come to life. I draw him in until I can no longer see, let him thrust a little farther and then when I think I can't drag any more pleasure from either of us, put one hand back on his balls, the other on my clit. Every pull has me gasping, wanting more. I back away—a red-eyed, drooling mess, and meet a gaze that isn't as fierce as I'd imagined, but hazy and lost. His cheeks are red, his eyes almost...soft. "I want to see you come. Wanna taste it."

He gives a quick nod.

With his blessing, I go to town—a glutton for new things, a glutton for *him*. I want his tastes, his pleasure on me, *in me*. I want to bathe in whatever he has to give. So I pull, hard, with my mouth, suctioning his flesh.

It's up and down, tight, skin to skin, want and want—too much, but I don't care. I don't care, because, when he loses his mind in my mouth, it's everything I could wish for.

He shoves me away, grasps his thick erection in his fist and works it, faster and tighter than I'd dared to. "Where do you want it?" he asks.

It takes me a second to understand what he means. When I do, I can't hold in a giggle. "I don't..." I laugh outright, turn, and kiss the tip of his erection. "Everywhere?"

He leans in, bright eyes eating me up. "You don't even know what it's..."

I kiss him, hard. "I do."

"Yeah?"

At my nod, his hand goes back to his cock, working it the way I want him to work my entire body—tight and quick and full of intent. His breath comes out in bursts.

I wait, rapt, as his eyes use me for pleasure, skimming over my face and breasts, down to where I'm rubbing myself, not as hard as he is, but just as fast.

"Oh, fuck, you filthy little slut."

"Yeah. Yeah, I am. With you. For you."

"Good." He meets my gaze. "Say my name."

"Karl." I'm breathing so hard, I almost can't push the sounds out. "I want you."

"Yeah." His breathing goes erratic, his eyes a little lost. He's close, and my God, I can't look away. When his left hand reaches for me, I shift close, giving myself over to his release.

I arch my body, offer it up to him.

He comes—*Oh, God, finally*—teeth gritted, jaw hard, eyes fierce and possessive.

The first spurt lashes my breast, then another, and another. I give up my own race to the finish and rub his spend into my skin, over my nipples, down to my belly. He growls, releasing one final pearlescent white jet onto his knuckles. Without thinking, I lean forward and lap it up.

Before I finish, he grabs me and hauls me onto his lap.

Karl

"I can't get enough of you," I mumble against her cheek, her ear, her mouth. I'm wrecked. "Just can't." My brain's too numb to produce coherent sentences. My arms wrap her up in a solid cocoon. It's all I have, right now, muscles and bones and whatever protection they give.

In the silence that follows, I fully recognize that this might be more than I'd bargained for.

She sighs, I tighten my hold. "Fuck, Jerusha. *Fuck.*"

"Agreed." Her laughter shakes us both. After a bit, she twists against me until I let her go enough to put us face to face. "Was that..." She bites her lip in an expression that I recognize as something like insecurity. "Did I do okay?"

The bottom falls out of my stomach. "Kidding me? Never felt this good in my life."

"So I did it right."

"Amazing." I smile. "We're good together."

Her lips curl up. "Told you."

And yeah, in this about-face, backward, opposite world, filth is beauty, obscenity's innocence, and our loss of control is the strongest bond I've ever forged with another human being.

It's not just sex. It's—

My mind goes blank when she stretches up and kisses me.

After a while—I don't know, a couple minutes? Long enough that I'm half-hard again—she makes one of those contented cat sounds and stretches. I want her, except this time it's not the pounding erection I've had the last few times we've been together, but the desire's there. I have a feeling it'll always be there when she's around.

Somebody's belly growls—hers, maybe. "Hungry?" I ask.

"Oh, yes. I've been working so hard to get the show ready, I keep forgetting to shop. And eat."

"I'll cook you dinner."

"Really?" Her eyes light up. "What will you make?"

I laugh, like really let go and laugh. "What do you *want* me to make?"

"Oh, something extremely fancy." After a moment of what appears to be deep thought, she yells, "Hotdogs!"

"Thought you said fancy."

"I was kidding."

"Kidding about fancy or hotdogs?"

"Surprise me. I'll eat whatever you make."

"Deal." We decide to meet back at my place at seven, which gives me time to run to the store while she can finally take the bath she'd been about to fill when I arrived. After a long, slow kiss that almost leads to another round, I head to the front door.

"Karl." She stops me, something different about her voice. "Would you, um...get condoms while you're out?"

I open my mouth to ask if she's sure and change my mind.

She's sure. I know that now. This woman knows what she wants.

And apparently that's me.

I nod with a wicked smile and take off before I undress her again.

20

ARE YOU GONNA GO MY WAY

JERUSHA

I'm at his door at seven sharp, carrying the throw I made for him and a bouquet I made up from stuff in my back garden. It's probably too much. Or not enough? Or weird?

Before I can talk myself into running the gifts back home, I knock. Squid woofs and Karl yells something. Even through the wood, the low rumble of his voice makes me shiver.

After a brief wait, he opens the door, letting a waft of garlicky air out. There's bacon, too. And spices, though I've no idea which ones. My mouth starts watering immediately, half from the food and half from the sight of him. Good gracious the man does things to me.

He looks clean and pressed, like he's just showered and put on fresh clothes. He maybe trimmed his beard, which is freshly squared off on his cheek and under his chin. I'll miss the stubble, but those angles are delicious. And the effort he's made blows me away.

Then there's his mouth. He must have trimmed around that, too. I can't stop staring at it. Thinking about what it can do.

"Jerusha." I've never liked my name so much as when he says it like that—resonating deep in his chest, with a pleased tilt to his lips.

"Karl."

"Come here." He pulls me to him, envelopes me—blanket and bouquet and all—and the world falls away. No more honking traffic, no more curious dog, no more worries that I'm doing things wrong or pushing too hard or wanting too much. Just pure, solid affection.

He smells like fabric softener and woodsmoke and dinner. When I bury my nose deeper into his chest, I smell the man beneath. After a last, big inhale, I pull back and present my gifts with a smile. "Is this okay? Flowers?" I shrug. "I picked things I thought you'd like."

He accepts the bouquet and looks at it closely. It's a bunch of green and brown objects—not just flowers, but seed pods and grasses and things that I've managed to grow or scavenge. After a second, his eyes meet mine. He's not smiling any more. At all. "I love it."

"Yeah? I also made this for you."

"When? In the past hour?"

I shrug again, unwilling to tell him that I made it a while ago, but never felt the confidence to give it to him.

The blanket's pretty simple—for me. It's a blend of browns and grey, wound together to make a forest of tree trunks. I pictured him throwing it over the porch swing. It would blend with the maple branches and the chain and the woodwork of the seat. Now, in his hands, I recognize that I'd pictured myself sitting under it. Maybe beside him.

Talk about projecting.

"If you don't like it, I can—"

"I do." He grips it tighter. "Thank you."

"You're welcome."

We stare at each other. I can't begin to guess what he thinks when he looks at me, but I see something so pure and real that it's almost religious. Gosh, that's silly.

No. No, maybe it's not. Maybe I need to stop thinking of religion as the thing my parents live and consider that it could be something rooted in the earth. In reality. Rooted in our bodies instead of lost in the ether.

"What's going on in your head?" he asks, making me wonder how long I've been watching him.

"I'm trying to figure out why I like you so much." *Love you.*

He barks out a laugh. "That's flattering."

"I don't mean there's nothing to like. There's a lot."

His smile seeps away, replaced with a fierce concentration. He opens his mouth and shuts it, takes a deep breath. "Come on through to the kitchen. I cooked."

I follow him down the hall, past his dark living room and what I thought would be a dining room, but actually looks like a workshop of some sort. I pause in the doorway.

"What's this?"

"My shop."

"I thought you were a restauranteur."

"That's my retirement." He eyes the crowded workspace. "This is... I don't know, my, ah, hobby? Meditation?"

"You work with wood?"

"And metal." He points toward the back of the house. "Metal shop's in the yard."

"Oh, right. I knew you did something noisy back there. Always wondered what you were up to."

"Mostly making chef's knives, but I'm branching out."

"Scissors?" I can't keep the excitement from my voice.

"Sounds like a challenge." He smiles, raises the blanket. "We can do a trade."

"The blanket's a gift. Let me pay you—"

"No." He steps close and bends down, putting his forehead to mine in that move that makes everything so tight and intimate. He's smiling. "Let me make you something."

Those words speak to my soul so deeply I almost can't believe I'm not the one who said them. Making things for people, with my hands, is my love language. The intertwined vines and branches and trunks on his blanket aren't just about the tree out front, they're about him. Deep roots, strong moral fiber.

"I'd like that."

"Me, too." He gives me a brief kiss—though my poor heart thrums wildly, expecting more—and ambles back to the kitchen.

I walk in and spin. "This is amazing!"

"You like?"

"I mean, it's like professional, right? Are you a chef?"

He shakes his head. "No. Worked in restaurants since I was fifteen. Dishwashing, prep, line cook..." He sets the bouquet down and stretches out a hand. Under the light, his scars shine like they've been plasticized. I want to kiss them, taste them. "I like working the front of the house. The bar. Talking to customers."

I like *you*, I want him to say, but this has all moved fast. Maybe he's not there yet. I swallow, hard.

It's fine. This is a lot. *I'm* a lot.

"Mind putting those in this?" He sets a vase on the granite counter. It's obviously hand-made, like every bowl I see. It's what I like about this room, even more than the stainless steel appliances, the massive cupboards, the pristine work spaces. There's art on every wall.

I fill the vase at the massive sink, half watching while he shakes a sizzling pan and checks on something in the oven. "Smells amazing."

He chuckles and turns to me. "I keep picturing you eating my food."

"Oh." I make a funny face and look side to side. "That's nice."

"Nice?" He throws a kitchen towel over his shoulder as he

moves in my direction, pushing his long sleeves over his elbows. It's like foreplay. I mean those forearms, they're lethal. I'm weak just looking at them. "There's nothing nice about the way I feel about you, Jerusha." His eyes flick to my mouth, then briefly down my body before rising to meet mine. "I want to taste you again." He sounds strangled; in pain.

"Oh." Understanding hits, in a flash. Good thing I'm not holding the vase of flowers or I'd drop it. My knees go weak, which is something I've only read about. If my hands were functional right now, I'd lift my skirt and offer myself up like a dish. Instead, all I can do is stand here and stare. We're breathing hard, not touching, not talking, just looking.

His brows crinkle, like there's something he's working hard to figure out. "Jerusha." Just my name sounds intense. I brace myself. "I—"

The oven timer shrieks, startling us both.

21

HOW SOON IS NOW?

KARL

"Shit."

Heart thumping hard enough to crack my ribs, I grab a mitt and take out the sweet potatoes, set the dish on the counter and toss the pan once before shutting the stove off.

"Fuck it." I turn to her, put my hands on the sides of her face and treat myself to the kiss I've been fantasizing about for the past two hours—in other words, forever. I show her my need in all its explicit glory.

She gives it right back, punctuated with grunts that have me digging deep for air—because I just can't stop. I don't fucking want to.

She's right. This is more than lust or sex.

My hands are everywhere, on her ass, in her hair, at her waist, her arms. And she's doing the same—pulling and stroking, and feeling me like I've never been felt. This isn't the urgency of a quickie, it's more extreme, like my life depends on getting close. I *have* to touch her. I need this and, Christ, she needs it back. She gasps when I pick her up and plop her on the counter, but she doesn't stop, she takes more. Gives more.

I've never felt a fraction of this for another woman. In this moment, I understand the thing I've been denying since the day I met Jerusha—I can't keep away.

She bites my lip and I groan, helpless to keep the sound in. My body slides between her legs, my crotch almost pressing to that hot, sweet juncture and I shut my eyes, going still, while she laps at me.

"I..." *Love you.* What is it about saying the words aloud that feels like doomsday?

Her expression's indescribably perfect—heavy-lidded excitement. Awe mixed with desire and affection, honestly, that's what does it. The look. How can I resist that combination?

After years of getting off on one-night stands or porn and my right hand, the way she wants me is a drug. The way I want her is *devastating*.

"I like that you're out of control...from being with me. I want that again. Seeing you come was..." She smiles, panting. "My favorite."

I let out a weak laugh and tighten my hold on her. "You're killing me."

"Will you come again?"

"Will *you*?" I stroke her thighs and she spreads them so I sink right into her, aching cock pressed to hot pussy. Her skirt's this thin, silky material. She nudges me back and gathers it above her knees. It's blue-green and looks like water pouring over her legs.

"I want to fuck you so bad, Jerusha."

"Do it," she gasps. "Do everything."

How easy would it be to rip my jeans open, tear her panties aside and sink in, fill her up with thick cock so she'll never need another? Never think of looking elsewhere? Shit, I could fuck her so long and so hard...

I meet her eyes and see none of the sunny innocence I'd

imagined that first day. There's joy, though, which is better. She *loves* this. And I love how unashamed she is. I'm twisting myself up in knots, while she's nothing but pure, fresh want. I'd say it's her most attractive feature, but it's impossible to narrow it down. Every bit of her's enchanting—her face, her body, her bright inner light.

I'm a goner.

Then she takes off her T-shirt. The blinds are up, but the only house with a view into this room is hers. "Watch out. Neighbor might see."

"Yeah?" Her smile's wicked. "She cute?"

"She's magnificent." My hand's at her throat—slender and precious. I glide down, smoothing slowly over collar bones, to the deep cleavage made by her pink cotton bra. I love that the bra and the skirt and shirt never match. I love that it's color over coordination. Joy over perfection. She doesn't give a crap what she's supposed to think or do or look like.

I ease the tips of my fingers under the top edge of the cup and glance up. Her smile's gone, her head's thrown back in open-mouthed pleasure. A jolt of pride hits me so hard I make a noise. Her eyes focus and meet mine.

Her lips curve.

And, fuck me, what am I doing?

I'm her first. She wants it, hell, *I* want it more than breathing. But being her first doesn't guarantee that I'll be her last. And that's the part I can't deal with.

22

SHE'S LOST CONTROL

JERUSHA

Every time we touch, I lose a piece of myself to love. To Karl. It's a strange thing, this confirmation that I've been right all these years: we're not just intellectual creatures, we human beings. We're physical. We're animals.

And I know that it's not the act that makes it good, it's the man. The scrape of rough calluses, the rasp of uneven breathing, the almost painful press of denim to my bare inner thigh—all of these are ways he shows me how he feels.

It's these details that make this so stunningly different from anything I've experienced. His fingers slide in, out, in again, never quite hitting my nipples. As if now that he's touched me there, he's in no hurry at all. That's belied by the sprinter's cadence of his breathing, the steady press and release of his hips into mine. The eager moans he lets out under his breath.

When he cups my entire breast, my hands shoot out to grasp whatever part of him they can, and pull. I need him close. In me. Filling me up, alleviating this ache.

"What is it, Dirty Girl?" He leans in, testing the weight of one breast, then the other. Back and forth, his eyes admiring his own work. Except I want to admire, too.

"Your shirt." I grab at the cotton, eager to touch him without it. "Can you take it off?"

Hurriedly, he pulls it up and over. And to say that I *like* what I see would be like saying that I eat for subsistence. I mean, I do, obviously, but food is so much more than energy.

This man is so much more than pretty.

"My God," I whisper, while my greedy hands stroke and knead. He speeds up after that—probably prodded by my reaction.

Efficient as can be, he reaches behind me and undoes my bra. My breasts drop out, loose and heavy and naked again. Although he's seen me like this before, his response is gratifying. He goes quiet—not breathing—and when his gaze lands on mine, he's shaking his head, eyes out of focus. "God, you really are beautiful."

One hand molds my breast, reverent and careful, when I'm aching for reckless.

"Harder."

His eyes, dark as ink now, linger on what his hands are doing. With a quick glance at my face and a glimmer of a smile, he shushes me, then looks back down, as if this were the most important job in the world. "Don't rush this, Jerusha." He pinches my nipple. "Let me enjoy you."

My head bobs acquiescence, slow and drugged by his attentions. Another pinch pushes a happy, pained gasp from my lips.

When he bends his head and puts his mouth to my tender skin, I'm lost, adrift in a sea of ecstasy. A lick, a nip, another lick, and then he sucks me in, like he can't get enough.

"Karl." His name escapes me in a pleasure-induced chant. "Karl."

He lets my nipple out with a pop and moves up. "Yeah," he says, before kissing me, deep and hard. There's ownership to this kiss—especially with the way he's playing down there. Tugging and flicking, caressing and pinching. "Wanna do this all night."

"Yes."

"But we'll be eating charcoal if I don't stop soon."

My mind clears, bringing with it the smell of searing meat and garlic. I blink at the room, surprised to see onion strewn across the floor. Beyond the windows, it's full dark.

"Wow."

He chuckles and leans in. "Yeah." Another kiss, more tender this time. More lips, less devouring with tongues. "We keep getting distracted like this, we'll both starve to d—" His eyes land on something over my shoulder and he curses. He's about to run to take care of whatever it is and stops to kiss one breast, then the other before carefully rehooking my bra and smoothing it. Which seems to distract him. But the smoke in the air's getting heavy.

"Save your meat!"

"Right." He races to grab the pan. "*Our* meat."

Squid, who's been sleeping against the back door lets out a low *Woof!* as if he knows exactly what's at stake here.

My feet drop to the floor and I slip back into my shirt as he transfers the pork to a cutting board and puts a piece of foil over it. He's grinding pepper onto the dish from the oven, then mixes up a salad, opens a bottle of wine and reaches for a couple glasses. "Here or the living room?"

"Whichever."

"Let's go in there."

After slicing the meat, he hands me plates and glasses. With Squid bringing up the rear, I follow him to the front of the house and set things up on the two-person table by the bay window. I sit and look outside at the windy night, feeling like I'm sitting in a restaurant.

Once we settle, with full plates and the dog sitting there staring, he pours the wine and holds up his glass. "You okay?"

I smile. "Better than okay."

"Good." He clinks his glass to mine with a funny expression. "Just want to make sure you're happy."

"I'm... Wait. What?" Why does this feel weird? "What do you mean?"

"Your first time. I want to do it right."

"Do it right? Is there a wrong way?"

"You forget the jackass on your porch?"

"Oh. True. What about you? Have *you* done it the wrong way?" My wine's still suspended in my hand, untouched. Images of Karl with other women run through my head and there are a *lot* in my imagination. The hot waft of food's suddenly not quite so appetizing.

He lets out a puff of air, his face wrinkling into a grimace. "Probably. No, definitely. There've been some not so great times."

"I'm sorry." My smile feels wooden, though I can't say exactly why.

"You going to drink that?"

"Oh. Yeah." I take a sip and set the wine down. It's good. A little chilled, which I hadn't expected from a red. And not as fruity as I'd expected. Which is fine. It's all fine. The setup, the food, the candle he's lit on the table between us.

But that's just it, it's a setup, isn't it? He's doing this to *help* me, not because he wants me, particularly, but because he doesn't want my first experience to be bad. And now that I've told him I love him... "You don't have to do this, you know, Karl."

Expressionless, he puts his fork and knife down, his movements careful and precise. "Excuse me?"

"You know, wine and dine me. I know you're just trying to make sure I'm not..." Oh, crud. How'd I even get into this conversation? "Nothing. You know what? Let's just enjoy ourselves."

"Isn't that what you want?" He's watching me closely. "To enjoy yourself?"

"Yes." I nod, once. "Yes. Yes it is."

"Good. And are you? Enjoying yourself?"

"Um. The food and..." I gesture vaguely at the table and then half turn toward the kitchen in back. "Or the..."

"Any of it. All of it. With me." He clears his throat. "It's...fun?"

Fun. Fun? Was this fun? It didn't feel fun. It felt...important. It felt real.

I open my mouth and shut it again, worried suddenly that I've done the wrong thing, following my emotions, even letting them exist, when he just means this as a favor. Helping out the new girl. The country bumpkin.

"You're...I, um... I appreciate it." I'm nodding, quick and awkward and smiling like I've put on a mask. "What you're doing for me." My body aches, sensitive and open. Still wet between my legs. It feels like a hangover, already. "I appreciate it," I choke out again, because I can't think of another thing to say. I grab my wine and drink it, fast. "Be right back."

I stand up and race to the bathroom, lock myself in, and collapse onto the toilet, hot face in my hands.

Karl

That went well.

Fuck!

I thump the table, which rattles everything. Squid sits up and gives me a look, as if to say, *What the hell man?*

Yeah. What the hell, man?

I stare out the window, where the trees are doing their best to shake off the last of their leaves. Even in the dark, the riot of colors stirs me up, reminding me of the woman who's just taken off for my bathroom. I should go after her, but I'm not sure what to say.

I'm fucking this up. Badly.

She was already upset tonight, about her parents and now trying too hard to make it right has shifted things toward wrong.

What should I do?

Hell, I don't know. I have no idea.

I grab my phone from my pocket and, before I can talk myself out of it, fire off a text.

Help me. I'm fucking up with Jerusha.

Who is this? And how'd you get my dad's phone?

Haha. I'm serious.

Admitting you're wrong? Hang on, Dad. Let me take a screen shot for posterity... Okay. What'd you do?

Asked if I was doing things right. You know, to her satisfaction.

Doing it right? Doing what right? Wait. No. Don't answer that. Forget I asked. Hold on. Is she with you?

Bathroom.

Hiding?

Shit, is she? I stand and head that way and then stop. I'm bad with women. Christ, I'm forty-three and I suddenly get this. I'm really, really bad at understanding them.

How do I make it right, Harper?

You're asking because you like her?

Yes. God, I don't just like her, Harper. I...

Holy shit, my life. Fuck-up dad asking his daughter for advice.

I'm falling in love with her.

Whoa.

Yeah. Whoa.

Tell her.

No.

Tell her.

It's too early.

Tell her. Tell her Tell her

I let my phone drop to my side, pick it up again, read the words, *falling in love,* then wait for the freak-out to arrive.

It doesn't. Instead, I type out another sentence and hit send, calm as I've been in my life.

I'm not falling. I love her.

And then, because I need to do better right now—maybe prove that I am a full-grown man—I go to the bathroom door. "You okay in there?"

"Yes. Yes, thanks." The sink goes on. I wait. Water keeps running.

"Jerusha. Are you hiding?"

The water goes off. "Maybe."

Shit. "I need you to know something."

Is she sniffing? Was she crying? Her *"Okay."* Sounds pretty doubtful, like maybe she doesn't want to hear what I have to tell her.

"I..." My head thunks lightly against the wood. "I think I have to tell you this in person. Face-to-face."

The knob turns, the door opens, and she's there, staring up at me with a huge smile. "Let's do this."

"What?"

"I want the next lesson."

I blink. "Now?"

"Good a time as any, right? It's time to have the sex." Her eyes skim down my front. "You got the condoms?"

"Uh... Yeah." I think about dinner on the table—mostly burned—and the wine I couldn't taste anyway. I think of what I admitted to Harper, but can't seem to say aloud. And then I think of how soft Jerusha's always been versus how thick her shell seems right now.

And that's my fault, 'cause I'm an idiot man who can't express his feelings...

To hell with that.

"I fucking love you, Jerusha." The words hurt on their way out, but my next breath comes easier than they have in a while.

Her expression's almost funny—a perfect mask of surprise. Then, slowly, a smile takes over her face. She looks so pure and happy in that moment the love's even stronger, filling up parts of me I hadn't known were empty.

"I love you," I say again. After a quick, hard kiss, I pull her into my arms. "You're right. Dinner can wait." I want her so bad, so deep inside. To hell with it—with a growl, I haul her up and over my shoulder, caveman style. "Now, let's go to bed."

She giggles the whole way up the stairs.

23

LET'S GO TO BED

KARL

I throw her on the bed in the near-dark of my room and follow her down. Every part of me is pounding with need.

Unable to wait another second, I yank off my shirt, drag my pants down, and remove my socks and underwear, watching as she eagerly undresses.

By the time we're both naked, I stand above her, blinking in the dark, just aching for her.

"What are you doing?" she whispers. "Is this the part where you regret the caveman bit and or telling me you love me?"

"No." I crawl over her and bend my arms to put our faces close, noses barely touching. "Fuck, you smell good."

"Sugar and spice?"

A harsh laugh presses our bellies together. "No. You smell like..." *Say it, asshole.* "Like the woman I've been waiting for. The woman I need. Like *my* woman."

I can't read her expression in the weak light from outside, but I hear her quick breathing. A second ago, I could think of nothing but getting inside her, but I won't do that to her. Not the first time, at least.

I lean to one side and skim the tips of my fingers from her forehead, over the bump of her nose, to her mouth. I almost expect her to lick me, but she doesn't. She just lays there, silent and still, like she knows I need this moment to learn her.

Hell, to learn myself.

I skim over her pointy chin and curved throat, between breasts I'll need to spend months getting to know. Maybe years.

"So fucking precious," I whisper, dipping into her belly button, then down, through wiry curls and lush, juicy labia, along one plush inner thigh, to the inside of her knee, over stubbled calf, sharp ankle, callused foot. Her toes are little, the nails textured, as if covered in layers and layers of polish, which I remember from this summer. Too impatient to take it off, she'd apply more. Colors, sparkles, wild designs.

I know this, because I paid very close attention to those little toes. I paid attention to everything. I just wouldn't admit it.

"You're not that macho," she says, partway through my return trip—with my mouth, this time.

I taste her hip, where bone and fat create a curve so artistic, I know something divine had a hand in its creation. My nose slides up to caress her waist. "Huh?"

"My friends say you're a macho, macho man."

I snort and she giggles. "Like the song?"

"The what?"

"Never mind." I drag my beard up her side, nudge her arm aside, and follow the line of her armpit—also stubbled—along her surprisingly muscular arm, to her hand. Her skin, stretched over tiny, delicate bones, is tough, her knuckles scarred, fingertips rough like mine. I kiss her, then slot my fingers between hers and tighten my hold, overwhelmed by something dark and protective.

"This thing between us, Jerusha." Christ, my voice is rough. "Scares the shit out of me."

Aside from a quick squeeze of her fingers, she doesn't move.

"See, I may have my shit together at forty-three, but you've done that at twenty-five. You know the value of things, you've had to fight to get where you are. You're young, but you're strong."

She nods, once.

"The thing is, sweetheart...I'm afraid." Air puffs out of my lungs, as if just saying it is a relief. "Afraid I'll make the same stupid mistakes. Afraid I'm not enough." I lean so close my words touch her ear. "See, I don't just want to be your first. I want to be your first and your last and everything in between. So, yeah, I love you. So much it scares the shit out of me."

"Say it again."

"You heard me. I love you, sweetheart."

Her teeth glow bright in the dim light. I want to lick that smile, to sip it up, to do whatever it takes to make it last forever.

"I think you like that I'm a stupid macho, macho man who needs time to work things out." I bop her nose with the tip of my index finger. "I think you like that I'm older, but not all that much wiser. I think you like having to fight for what you want. So maybe, just maybe you'll understand that I needed to fight for you, too. In my messed-up man way."

"By fight, you mean sling me over your shoulder and haul me upstairs?" Her voice is high and light, but I don't think the question's as off-hand as it seems. "Or is that the deep internal struggle you've dealt with this week?"

"Listen, you're so open to things, so ready to do and see and explore. Jerusha, you've gone on more dates in the last few months than I have in ten years."

"That's 'cause you're boring."

"Cautious."

"Boring.

"And yet, you love me."

"Touchée." I hear her smile.

"You, Jerusha Graff, are fucking irresistible. You're wide-eyed and wide-open. You grab life by the throat, you suck it all in and you *live*. It's the most honest, most...*glorious* thing I've ever seen. And here I am, trudging along, trying to get things right the what? Fourth time around?"

She gasps. "Are you thrice divorced?"

"Just the once. But, unlike you, I've had my share of failed relationships."

"You scare me, too." She rubs her face to mine, the move luxurious. "But in the best way."

"Listen." I shift my bottom half closer, let her feel my hard cock and the shuddering breath I suck in. "I'm done protecting myself. If fear's set off my fight or flight, I'm going all out, tooth and nail. I'll fight anything that gets in our way. You mean that much to me." The words are too intense for a first talk like this, but they're out now. Too goddamn late. "You woke up the caveman, Jerusha. I'll take on anyone who hurts you or tries to keep us apart."

"Good thing Harper likes me." She clears her throat. "I think."

"Thank fucking God." I kiss her cheek. "And me. Don't forget. I like you."

"You more than like me."

"I fucking love you." What a relief to say it again, to recognize this thing that's been torturing me for so long. "Adore you. With every cell in my body."

"And soul."

"Yeah." I nod, my chest expanding with all the emotion. "Almost hurts. Now open your legs."

She blinks "What?"

"We've got a lesson to get through."

"Are you saying having sex with me's some kind of chore for you?" There's a laugh in her voice. It's addictive. "Just another chore to complete? A milestone to—"

"No. I'm saying lie down..." I rise up again, knee her thighs apart, and drop my pelvis. And then, because I suspect it's what she wants, I lower my voice and whisper in her ear, "So I can fuck you, you little slut."

Jerusha

Oh my God. It's happening. We're doing it.

And he loves me.

I'm buzzing—every little part of me, including my insides. I could laugh or cry or throw my head back and scream.

When Karl makes his way down my body again, shoves me open, and licks my sex, I groan—from equal parts pleasure and impatience. "Nooooooo."

He lifts his head, throws one of my legs over his shoulder and smirks up at me. "No?"

"I mean, yes, but...I want to do the other thing."

"You want me to fuck this pretty little pussy?" He slides a finger inside me and everything clenches tight

"Yes, please."

"Say it like you mean it." He licks me, long and slow, as if he's got all the time in the world, when really I'm about to burn up with need. "Convince me."

"I want your big cock in my tight little pussy," I force out. And then, because just saying it made me warmer and heavier and more excited, I pinch my nipples and go on. "I want you to stretch me out." The words flow from me, filthy and wrong and so utterly right. "I want you to fill me up. Use me."

With a curse, he's up and off the bed, pulling a plastic bag from his drawer. He empties it onto the blanket, grabs one of the boxes, which he opens and then fights with one of the flat packages that emerge.

I watch, rapt, as he drags a condom down his thick length.

Everything about him is mesmerizing, from the bulky silhouette of his thighs in front of the window, to the flexing of his hands and forearms and the efficient way he deals with his own body. I love how his head's bent in concentration. I love the tight pull he gives himself before settling back on top of me with a heavy sigh.

And, goodness do I love the warm, solid press of him before he shifts back, reaches down, and works himself against me. The sound of his cock running between my soaked lips is so sexual, I shiver. This. This, right here, is the thing I've wanted for so long.

Well, one of them.

He notches himself at my entrance, drawing a gasp from my lips, looks up and goes still. "Might hurt."

I bite my lip and nod. "I know."

"I'll go slow."

"I know."

He leans forward, as if to show me with his tongue just how slow and explicit he can be.

And then he's pushing in. The pressure's strange, foreign, despite the fact that I've used toys before. Part of it's his closeness and his heat, but there's another thing about it that I can't quite put my finger on. The inexorability, maybe. Although that's not quite right. He'll stop if I want him to.

But I don't.

Of their own volition, my hands dig into his bottom, my hips move—away or toward him, I'm not even sure.

"That's it," he mutters. "Take it."

Oh, and it's dirty when he talks like that. I tighten around him, he groans, head dropping low, and goes still. "You're gonna kill me, sweetheart."

I can't talk, but my hips move. My hands urge. The slight discomfort is giving way to something hungry, something urgent. "More," I whisper.

He pushes in and I freeze, suspended. Waiting. For pain? For pleasure?

I'm full, pinned to the bed, and ready, though I don't even know what for.

"I want more."

With a groan, he pulls out and presses forward again—I feel every inch of him sliding in and the friction's like nothing I've experienced. "Again."

Another long, slow withdrawal, another languid penetration. He goes again and again, twisting me up inside, while I urge him on. Quickly, we move into new territory, words fly from our mouths, though I can't tell what they mean. Doesn't matter as much as the feel of hot breath and dark desire. He's pounding into me now and I'm holding him to me, fingers digging into thick muscle to prod him on.

He slows, leans back, and moans, low and guttural. "Look. Look at us. Look at how deep I am."

I lift my head to see what he means and go faint at the flash of wet cock, working me like a piston.

"Oh, yeah, that's it. Just like that. Clamp on, baby. I wanna fill you with my come. I wanna fill you, wanna fuck you so hard."

"You are. You are, Daddy."

"Fuck." His eyes land on mine. He looks lost. Sweaty and intense and absolutely wrecked. "Fuck, Jerusha. Fuck, this is..." His slick forehead drops to grind against my shoulder. I turn and kiss him. Any part of him, whatever I can reach.

"Gonna come, sweetheart." He's breathing so hard it's got to hurt. "Want to bring you with me."

"Yeah. Yeah."

He shifts again, reaches down and slides his hand between our slippery bodies and—

I scream. The sound is dragged from my soul, along with the dark, wrenching pleasure of this orgasm. All I can do is hold on to his wide shoulders and let it take me—let him take me—to the deepest reaches of myself.

And my God, it's beautiful.

I'm just coming down when he reaches his own completion, shouting and thrusting hard three final times, holding himself inside me like he never wants to leave. When he finally emerges and raises his head, there's the sweetest smile on his face.

"So fucking perfect," he mumbles halfway through a messy kiss. He's just deepened it when my belly growls. With a laugh that sounds pained, he pulls out of my body, leaving me happy and sore and a little bereft. "Let's get you fed, woman."

24

ABOUT A GIRL

Two Weeks Later...

Karl

"So, what's the plan?" Harper asks as we pull into the farm's drive.

"No idea. Knock on the door. Hope for the best."

"Dad."

I throw up a hand. "Look, this is new to me, okay? I'm just trying to make her happy."

"Your girlfriend."

I open my mouth and shut it. How can I explain to my daughter that Jerusha's not just my girlfriend, she's my fucking soul mate? Every second with her, every step we take, confirms it.

And, since I've never been the kind of guy who believes in shit like soul mates, it's not easy to talk about.

I cast my daughter a look, find her staring at me in a funny way, and sigh. "What?"

"This is it for you, isn't it? She's it?"

I shrug, and then regret it, because there's no I don't know about it. "Yep. She's it. My person."

"And she feels the same."

I throw my daughter a look. "That a question?"

"Nope." She shakes her head. "I hear everything from Mikey. You guys are for real."

I can't keep the grin from my face. Why the hell should I when there's nothing but truth? Nothing but good in my life?

Which is why I'm here today, in the Shenandoah Valley, pulling up to the pretty brick-red farmhouse that Jerusha grew up in. The place is picture-perfect, with its pristine white trim, surrounded by barns, grazing cows in the distance.

I'm here because this is the one rough patch in our existence. These people have thrown away my woman's love and I'm not okay with it.

"Ready?" Tension ticks in my jaw

I meet Harper's eyes and she's young and smiley and dressed as primly as she knows how. "As ever."

We get out and head to the porch. There's a handful of invitations burning a hole in my coat pocket. Whatever happens today, those are staying here.

There's no question that the woman who answers the door is related to Jerusha. Her hair, for starters, wisps out of the tightly-pulled bun, as if she'd like to get it under control, but can't. Her blue eyes—also like her daughter's—take me in and go from curious to wary. Which is exactly why I brought Harper.

"Afternoon, ma'am." If I wore a hat, I'd take it off. Anything to seem like an upstanding guy. Like the type of man who deserves a woman like Jerusha. "I'm Karl McCoy and this is my daughter Harper. We're, ah, here because..." I swallow, still unsure of what I'm doing. No. I'm unclear on how to do this, but I know it's the right thing. And that's what makes me pull the invites from my pocket and hand them to her. She takes them, unhesitatingly, and then seems unsure of what to do with them.

"Those are for you. From Jerusha."

"Oh!" Her eyebrows lift, her features go wide and bright. She looks behind me, as if searching for her daughter. Her eagerness twists something in my belly.

"I'm sorry. She's not here, I've just... Listen, Mrs. Graff, when she got the invite back in the mail, she was pretty upset."

"I don't... What do you mean?"

"This show's a huge deal for her. For her career. She's the youngest artist to have a solo exhibit of this size at the Werner Gallery and she really wanted you to be there."

She squints down at the postcard. "I've never seen this."

"She sent you one. It was returned."

Mrs. Graff puffs out a breath, which seems to deflate her, chest-first. She's a fairly tall woman, maybe in her late fifties or early sixties, with rosy cheeks and smile lines around her eyes and mouth. Right now, though, she looks drawn and sad. A little hollowed out. "He sent it back?"

I open my mouth, consider placating her and decide to go with the truth. "Your husband. Yes."

"All right. Well, um. Thank you." She takes a hold of the door, as if to close it and then maybe realizes this isn't the polite thing to do. Looking shaken, she drops her arms, half-turns, and waves at the dark, still house behind her. "Would you care to come in for a—"

"No," I interrupt, though I'd love to see where Jerusha grew up. The invitation's clearly half-hearted. I share a look with Harper, who gives a quick shake of her head. "Thank you. We've got a couple hours on the road and... We'll let you get back to..." I don't even know what to say. Life? That seems cold.

Thankfully, Harper steps in to help. "Thank you so much, Mrs. Graff, but Dad and I need to head back. For Jerusha's art opening. It's today. Have a great afternoon, okay?" Her smile's so warm, so genuine, that I can't help feeling pride. Not that I can take credit for how sweet she is, but I can appreciate it.

We say our goodbyes and get back in the truck, without another word. We're halfway up the driveway when Harper tells me to stop. "Take me back."

"Why?"

"I want to give her my number. In case she needs to get in touch."

I nod, impressed that she thought of that. I pull a three-point turn and park, then watch from the truck as she charms Jerusha's mother.

"I'm proud of you, Harper," I tell her when she's back in the truck.

Her eyebrows fly up. "Yeah? Why?"

"You're a good person."

"Well, I can thank you for that."

I shake my head. "I'm proud, but I had nothing to with making you this way."

"You're an idiot." She snorts, shakes her head, rolls her eyes, and turns to look out the window, but not before I see the emotion on her face. "Now, get me that ice cream you promised."

I reach out, squeeze her hand, happy when she squeezes back, and sniff, fully aware of who's responsible for the stuff I've been feeling lately.

Jerusha Graff, the love of my life. I can't wait to get back to Richmond to tell her how much I adore her, how much she's changed me. For the millionth time this week.

With a sigh and an eye-roll of my own, I put the car in drive. I'm about to start for home when something slams in the distance. "Dad, hold on!" Harper says, pointing at the two women on the front porch. "Looks like we've got company."

25

FLOAT ON

JERUSHA

The doors opened half an hour ago and Karl is nowhere in sight. He should have been here earlier. He promised he'd be at my side all night.

I swallow, hard, and plaster a smile on my face, though I'm worried. This isn't like him. And, aside from a text earlier, telling me to get ready for a big surprise, I've heard nothing from him all day.

Also not like him.

"Hey, doll face!" Mikey comes up beside me, wearing a massive grin.

"Mikey!" I let them wrap their arms around me, so relieved to have them here. "You made it."

"Of course I made it. Was I not supposed to come to my bestie's opening?" They look around, eyes huge. "In case you haven't noticed. You're kind of a big deal."

I can't help but laugh. It's not true, but it feels good. And having them with me feels good, too. "Have you heard from Harper?"

"Um... Yes." Mikey goes all cagey. "And Alba's here! She's talking to someone outside."

I narrow my eyes. "What's going on?"

"I've been sworn to secrecy."

"Am I going to like it?"

"Sure hope so. Hey, come here." I accept the hug, though I know the risk of crying is high. It's nerves and emotion and a big dose of exhaustion. To hell with what everyone thinks. I'm an artist, after all. I'm allowed to cry at my first big opening. I let it go —just a little. A couple tears escape my eyes, I sniffle. After a couple silent snuffles, I wipe my eyes and pull back. "Thank you."

"Stop saying that." They lean forward and wipe under my eyes. "Now, go talk to your adoring fans."

With a nod and a deep breath, I paste on a smile and turn back to the room.

A couple minutes later, Alba shows up, then a couple of my professors. But no Karl.

Time's weird during events like this—especially now that I'm the main attraction. It passes in fits and starts, rushing until it's time for me to give my speech—the part I've been dreading. I'm fine talking to people, although accepting compliments is still a challenge, but standing up in front of a crowd will be a whole other situation.

Darn it, I really wanted him to be here.

I stand stiffly through the Collection Director's introduction and move to the little stage they've set up in the lobby.

Once I'm up there, I start to shake—nerves, I suppose. It's not like I've done this before. After a big inhale, I dive into my prepared artist's talk.

"Thank you." I clear my throat. "This show is called *Pieces of You* because it's a collection of my past. Bits and pieces of who I am. The good, the bad..." My hand waves to a massive, dark piece hanging on the right. "The ugly." There's laughter.

Okay. Okay, I can do this. I'll get through it. I don't need Karl. He'll get here when he can. And whatever he's doing, he's got good reason for it. "We're all made up of our past, our present, genetics, learned behaviors and experiences. Everything you see on these walls is something I've seen or been or lived. It's the best of where I grew up." I sniff. "And the worst." I keep talking and after a minute, maybe longer, I start to focus in on the people standing here and, my goodness, there are a lot. Hundreds. I skim over the crowd, touching on one face and another. Toward the back, a tall figure attracts my notice. I blink and lose track of what I'm saying. I take a breath. "It's disappointment...and *happiness*." That last word comes out close to a whisper. It's Karl, back there. He's here. He made it.

With a shaky inhale, I turn to the rainbow creation I've put together over the past couple weeks—an ocean of color and texture. It's the most complex piece I've ever made, and the most personal. I clear my throat, unsure of where I am in the speech. It doesn't matter, I guess. I'm not a public speaker, after all, I'm a just a woman who likes to knit. "Sometimes, I'm not even sure of what it is that I'm making," I admit, which will probably cost me some sales, since art's supposed to be all about meaning and insight, right? "Sometimes, the process is as important as the product." I look back to him. To Karl. To the man I love, who's pushing his way through the crowd like a moving stone through still water.

Who am I even talking to now? What am I even saying?

I open my mouth to say something else and lose the thread when I realize Karl's not the only one moving toward me. He's the engine of a long train, cutting its way through the crowd. There's Harper and... I hiccup. Is that my mother? And Rachel, my little sister? Behind her, my other siblings approach, all of them watching me as I stutter at the front of the room.

Full of emotion, I muster a deep breath and find my voice

again. "This show, all of it, every filament, knot, and thread, is the sum total of my parts. The pieces of me."

"Thank you," I force out, overcome by dizziness as I step away from the mic to a surprisingly stupendous round of applause. That made no sense. Why are they clapping?

Probably because it made no sense. Eccentric artist speak.

Someone comes up to congratulate me, followed by another person I've never met. I'm surrounded by art buffs and philanthropists, professors, students. I smile and nod and give thanks and react when someone tells me they've decided to buy three pieces, and then turn and Karl's there.

He nods.

I press my lips together, folding them in on each other. It's all I can manage with all the emotion swelling inside.

"Hello, Jerusha." I turn toward the voice.

"Hi Mama." Tears blur my vision.

"I'm so proud of you." Her last word is a whisper that I feel more than hear as she pulls me in close. Mama's smell, the soft feel of her hair against my cheek, the busy way her fingers tighten against my back in little spasms she can't control. "So happy you did it. You became..." She pulls back and looks around, then at me. "Yourself."

I nod and force a smile. It's tough with all these feelings so close to the surface. It would be easier to grimace. I lean in to hide against her shoulder, turn and push my face into her neck.

It takes a while for my siblings to cycle by and tell me they're so happy for me and they knew I'd make it. I had no idea they felt this way—no notion that they were proud or wanted this for me. It hurts and feels good, so mixed up I can hardly feel the disappointment at Papa's absence.

When Karl finally makes it back, I'm wrung out. His forehead presses to mine, bringing those big, dark, ferocious eyes in close.

"Thank you, Karl."

He rubs our noses together. "I'm gonna give you space right now, so everyone else can congratulate you, but...just remember: I'm yours. For here. For now. As long as you want me."

I'm breathing hard and fast. It's hard to get words out. "To do with as I please?" I whisper.

His reply, a pained-sounding chuckle, warms my lips. "Whatever you want. Anything. For now and the foreseeable future."

"Okay." I smirk. "Get ready for it, then..." My mouth makes its way over his cheek to his ear. "*Daddy.*" I give him one final look before pulling away, intent on doing as he suggested—talking to everyone, spending time with the family he's brought back to me, soaking up this feeling of a job well done. And making him wait his turn.

Then, when we're alone again—which might not be for a while—I'm going to show him just how happy he's made me.

EPILOGUE

Last Kiss

FIVE MONTHS LATER...

Karl

I swipe the sweat from my eyes and open the gate to see Jerusha on her hands and knees, planting more seeds in her veggie garden.

"Finished," I tell her, testing the hinges a couple times.

"Yaaaaaay!" She jumps up, clapping, and runs over to throw herself in my arms. As her legs wrap around me, I slide my hands under her ass and anchor her in place. We do this a lot. Glee's an everyday occurrence with my woman and I love it. After sprinkling a dozen kisses on my face, she nuzzles my ear. "I love it."

"I love you," I reply, surprising no one.

Her giggle's my favorite sound. Well, second favorite. I really like the way she sighs when my cock slides deep inside her. And the little noise she makes when she stretches first thing in the morning, before her eyes even open, or the happy song she sings when she eats my food.

Hell, I love every goddamn thing she does. Like now, she's sort of rubbing her tits against me, like the dirt and sweat doesn't matter. Which it doesn't.

We're in our backyard—shared, now that I've put the gate in —and I'll fuck my woman if I want to. Course, my dirty girl reads my mind. In fact, judging from the long, loose dress she's wearing, she clearly read my mind while putting her clothes on this morning, because once I've pulled my cock from my pants, there's not a barrier between us. She shimmies until the silky fabric's pooled around her waist, leans back, and reaches for me.

I look down at the strange feel of her hand on my cock, and burst out laughing at the sight of her gardening gloves. It takes her a second to realize what she's done. One of her bright, addictive giggles bursts out of her and I don't even try tamping down the caveman instinct. It's pretty constant around her. Thank God she's into being smashed against doors and onto floors and hauled up onto sinks and fucked, hard, because I'd die if we didn't have this.

With a sweet little growl, she yanks off the gloves and throws them down before shifting her weight, grabbing my dick, and notching it right at her entrance.

We stop, bodies frozen, breath held, eyes connected. I don't have to tell her again, but I want to. "Love you."

"Me, too," she whispers.

"You're everything."

"No, you are." Her lips curve, just the slightest bit.

Giving in—*finally*—I tighten my ass, thrusting slowly into her. Each hot inch is like the first time. Like every time. *We're everything*, is my last coherent thought before the beast takes over.

Cock pounding, every muscle working, I take her. Pumping my hips, bouncing her body on mine, watching the way she rubs her clit until she's close. Her cunt grips me, her eyes roll back and I clench hard, push deep inside, and let go.

Slowly, my brain comes back. I come back to the early spring-time hum of birds and passing cars, music blaring from open windows. After a long kiss, I pull out and put her on her feet, only removing my hands when I know she can stand on her own.

She does a funny little dance to make the skirt drop and I wonder, not for the first time, if she'll ever change her mind about getting married.

"You're doing it again," she says, half-glaring, half smiling.

"What?"

"Don't ask me. Don't do it."

"I won't. I promised and I meant it."

"Thank you."

I nudge her nose with mine, smiling at how she read my mind. And it's fine. Marriage isn't what matters. It's her. It's this. Us.

This gate between our yards was her idea. It's practical, given that we spend every single night together. I figure she'll ask me to take the whole damned fence down by summertime.

But it's her call. Every step, she gets to decide. Every choice is hers. She knows how I feel, after all. I'm an open book. I'm hers, hook, line, sinker, and the goddamn boat we sailed in on.

Anything she wants is hers, including me.

Especially me.

"I love you, Karl," she whispers.

"Love you, Dirty Girl."

THE END

EXCERPT FROM UNCHARTED

Coming 2021

Slowly, he lowered himself to the ground, full of the smell of rotting leaves and mud, fresh green growth in there somewhere, though it had yet to pop. She followed him down, pointedly ignoring the way he watched her—like if he blinked she'd disappear—and got to work.

Instead of shutting his eyes through the painful application of antiseptic, he kept them wide open, losing focus in the treetops halfway through the bandaging process.

"Lift."

He obeyed, held himself up while she wrapped a bandage around his middle, and settled back down, waiting for her to finish.

Which took forever. Her hands smoothed the tape, her fingers tested the edges, lingered...

When his surprised gaze met hers, there was a challenge in her expression.

Somewhere far away, the helicopter's engine growled, back

within earshot again. Or maybe it was just that his ears suddenly worked again.

He ignored it. Not blinking, not breathing. Just waiting, watching, his skin prickling, antsy with cold and anticipation.

The air was different, muskier, more alive than it had been in forever—with movement and scents, sounds, and a light, chilly breeze. Birds cawed to the west, just over the crest of this mountain, while the aircraft circled back from the east. They'd have to land on top of him to get him to move right now.

"Do it." His voice was a raw, open thing, more vulnerable than the wound she'd just covered. Want wasn't something he allowed himself. Wasn't much point when everything worth wanting was out of reach.

Only it wasn't right now. It was right here. And he couldn't remember wanting like this—ever.

He put out his hand, let his fingers curve around her dark, perfect ear, let them drag along the soft skin. He gently pinched the lobe, testing its softness, before cupping her ear again, the fleshy part of his palm flush with her jaw.

Her eyelids dropped, opened, stayed at half-mast, and then, like a dream he'd wake up to feeling empty and lost, she pushed back, giving him the weight of her head, the curve of her cheek.

She lowered her head.

"One kiss." The words were a hot breath on his belly, fanning his hair, tightening his abs.

Instead of rising over him and planting those lips on his, she dipped, paused, burned a path over his skin with her eyes, then pressed her mouth right where his pants ended low on his hips.

Look for UNCHARTED in May 2021. Visit adrianaanders.com/uncharted for more information.

ACKNOWLEDGMENTS

You know when someone does something and it sets off a chain of events? I'd been thinking for a while about writing a sexy, short book just for fun; a palette cleanser between the big, emotional books. Well this book didn't end up being the quick work I'd imagined, but it did made me happy along the way—and it taught me so much. I'm so happy you came along for the ride.

I've got a lot of people to thank for this book, beta readers and hand-holders and friends and inspiration. Thank you, first of all, to Katee Robert for inspiring me to just do it—to write the thing running around in my head.

Thank you to Leigh Kramer for beta-reading the hell out of this book and giving a thoughtful, deep critique. It made all the difference. Alleyne Dickens, Megan Frampton, and Alexa Day, thank you for reading (sometimes many versions of) Daddy Crush and helping me make it what it is. Thank you to Kimberly Cannon for being the most patient copy editor to walk this earth. You're a pleasure to work with, as always. Jennifer Seay, of Mercurial Forte, I LOVE this cover. A million thank yous (again) to Alleyne Dickens for being with me every step of the way with this book and all of the others that didn't make the final cut, and to Kasey Lane for listening to every single lament, every day. You two were my pit crew, my cheerleaders, and my shoulders to lean (cry) on. Love you guys.

To Amanda Bouchet, Tracey Livesay, and Andie J. Christopher—I'm so lucky to have you.

Finally, to you, my readers, who've followed me down one more new path: you guys are the best. I wouldn't be here without you.

ALSO BY ADRIANA ANDERS

The Love at Last Series

Loving the Secret Billionaire

Loving the Wounded Warrior

Loving the Mountain Man

The Survival Instincts Series

Deep Blue

Whiteout

Uncharted - Coming in 2021!

The Blank Canvas Series

Under Her Skin

By Her Touch

In His Hands

ABOUT ADRIANA ANDERS

Adriana Anders is author of the Survival Instincts, Love at Last, and Blank Canvas series. Her debut, Under Her Skin, was a Publishers Weekly Best Book of 2017 and double recipient of the HOLT Medallion award, and Loving the Secret Billionaire was a Romance Writers of America 2019 Rita® Award Finalist. Her books have been featured in Entertainment Weekly, Oprah Mag, Bustle, USA Today Happy Ever After, and Book Riot. Today, she resides with her husband and two small children on the coast of France, where she writes the gritty, emotional love stories of her heart. Visit Adriana's Website for her current booklist: adrianaanders.com

adrianaanders.com/newsletter
facebook.com/adrianaandersauthor
twitter.com/AdrianasBoudoir
instagram.com/adriana.anders